Teddy is focused on one thing, and one thing only — making his brother proud. That means finishing his Master's degree with the highest grades possible, then finding a good job. Those plans don't leave time for anything else, so when Teddy is told he needs a date for a birthday party, he lies and says he has one in the hopes that he'll be able to wiggle his way out of the party.

He doesn't.

Instead, he finds himself having to come up with a fake boyfriend, and he has no idea who can help him with that, so he's lucky Sterling, a Gillham pack member and one of his acquaintances, comes up with someone.

When a pack member approaches Ollie and asks him if he wants to play fake boyfriend for a friend of his, Ollie agrees. He hopes it will help distract him from the jealousy he feels at the sight of his best friend with his mate. He loves Gabriel and Gabriel's new mate, but he wants what they have, and he doesn't know how to get it.

They're both stunned when they meet at the party and realize they're mates. Teddy doesn't have time for Ollie, but can he really give up his only chance at being with his mate? And can Ollie get over what his parents did to him and trust Teddy, especially when Teddy is trying so hard to keep him at arm's length?

Ollie
Copyright © 2020 Catherine Lievens
ISBN: 978-1-4874-2798-6
Cover art by Angela Waters

Published by eXtasy Books Inc or
Devine Destinies, an imprint of eXtasy Books Inc

Look for us online at:
www.eXtasybooks.com or www.devinedestinies.com

OLLIE
WYOMING SHIFTERS: 12 YEARS LATER BOOK 10

BY

CATHERINE LIEVENS

CHAPTER ONE

A loud crash made Teddy jump in his seat. He scowled at the door, but even though it was closed, he could still hear what was happening outside.

Nysys was getting ready to throw a party, and everyone in the house knew it.

How could they not? Nysys was always noisy, but he got even noisier when he was focused on something, especially something like a party. Teddy wished he could tell the man to stop, but he couldn't. Nysys had just as much right as him to organize a party. They were both Whitedell pride members, and that was that. It didn't matter that Nysys was disturbing Teddy's studies. It didn't matter that he was making as much noise as a herd of elephants. Teddy and the rest of the house just had to deal with it.

The door flew open. Teddy was hiding in the living room, but he should have known that wouldn't last for long. He'd needed a change of pace, though, after spending the past few days in his bedroom.

Nysys paused at the entrance for a second, then strode inside. Teddy's shoulders slumped. There was no way he was studying now. "What do you need?" he asked Nysys.

Nysys grinned at him as if he didn't realize he was disturbing Teddy. He probably didn't, actually. He was so focused on his party that he didn't understand how much he was bothering everyone. "I was just going to start decorating the living room."

Teddy frowned. "Decorating? It's still days before the

party."

"And I need everything to be perfect."

Teddy leaned back against the couch and scowled. "This isn't your mate's first birthday party. Why do you need everything to be perfect? Why do you even need to throw him a birthday party in the first place? He's going to live more than a hundred years. Couldn't you skip the party this year?"

Nysys arched a brow and crossed his arms over his chest. "Someone is grumpy."

"You would be grumpy, too, if you were trying to study and someone kept making noise and disturbing you."

A flash of guilt passed on Nysys' face, but it was gone fast. "Well, I'm sorry I'm disturbing you, but some of us have more in our lives than books."

"I know that. But it's important for me to—"

Nysys waved. "Of course it's important for you to do well in your studies. I know that. And I'm sorry if I'm disturbing you. But you need to relax sometimes, Teddy."

"I do relax." Rarely. But Teddy had better things to do than relax. He needed to focus on his studies and doing well. He owed it to his brother, Jayden.

"Are you sure? Because some days, it looks like there's nothing in your life but school. And I get it. You want to make your brother proud and to make it in life. That's great. But you're still a kid. You have time, probably more so than my mate has birthdays. You could take a year off or something."

The thought horrified Teddy. "I'm not taking a year off from my studies."

"Fine, then take a few *hours* off. Surely you can do that? Maybe you could help me with the party."

Teddy shook his head. "I'm sorry. I'm just too busy." And he had no sense of aesthetics. If he decorated, it would probably look like a party supplies store had vomited all over the place. "I'm going to go upstairs."

Nysys shrugged. "Whatever. But remember, all work and no fun—"

Teddy rolled his eyes. "I *have* fun. I just don't like the same things as you. I like books and serious stuff."

"You're right. I don't find books fun. That doesn't mean I'm stupid." There was a hint of anger in Nysys' voice, and that was the last thing Teddy needed. The last thing he wanted, too.

He didn't want to offend anyone. He liked Nysys most of the time. The man was great, even though he was weird, and Teddy had grown up with him in his life as if he were an uncle or something.

But Nysys was right. Teddy was trying to make his brother proud, and that wouldn't happen if he slacked off and didn't graduate. "I'll think about it, okay?"

Nysys wrinkled his nose. "I don't think that thinking about it is enough. Look, you've been studying for days. We've barely seen you during meals, let alone the rest of the day. Why don't you take a few hours off? It won't hurt your studies. If anything, it will help you relax, and you'll probably be able to study more once you are."

Teddy hesitated. He wanted to think that Nysys was right, but he wasn't sure he could risk it. He wasn't a party guy. When he went to parties—something that didn't happen often—he was the guy who hung out in corners and against the walls. He was the guy people forgot was there. And sometimes that hurt, but he was aware that it was because of the way he behaved.

He loved the pride. The pride and its members had been his family ever since he was a teenager. With them, he'd found something he'd thought he'd lost forever after his mother had died. He'd gotten his brother back, and so much more. He might not have lived with the pride until recently when he'd moved out of his brother's house, but this had still been his family, and it was where he'd spent most of his Christmases and Thanksgivings.

But he should have remembered how messy holidays could be. Before he moved in, he thought that this place was a mess because he was only here for family celebrations. That wasn't right, though. Now that he'd lived here for several years, he knew that the house was never quiet. There was always someone doing something, usually Nysys or Keenan. There was always a party being organized, or a play date with all the kids. The house never slept, never slowed down, and once again, Teddy wondered if he'd done the right thing by moving here.

He could have stayed with his brother and his mate, but he needed some space. He was an adult now, and Jayden had already given enough of his life to him. He'd raised Teddy since he was thirteen, and he and Heath deserved to start a life alone as a couple.

So Teddy didn't have another place to go, and he didn't really want to leave. His love for the pride would never change, even though he wished that sometimes things were a little quieter and calmer.

Nysys rubbed his face. "I'm sorry. I just want you to be happy." His face lit up, and Teddy knew Nysys had thought of something he wouldn't like. He didn't usually like Nysys' ideas. No one did, not even his mate.

Nysys' smile widened. "I'll find you a date."

Teddy blinked, needing a few seconds to make sense of the words that had just passed Nysys' lips. "Date?"

Nysys looked like he pitied Teddy. "You know what a date is, right? It's when you bring someone to a party? When hopefully you at least kiss them, but I hope you'll do more than that. I'm pretty sure you need to get laid. The fact that you haven't been in a while is probably behind how stressed you are, and that needs to change. Well, and how much studying you've been doing. You really need to slow down when it comes to all of that."

Teddy didn't want to date. If it was up to him, he wouldn't even come to the party. He didn't have to, but it was an event for the entire pride, and eventually, someone would notice he wasn't there. He might be good at hiding in corners, but that didn't mean people didn't notice him at least once or twice during a party. Especially if Jayden was coming, come to think of it. He probably was. He and Heath lived on the ranch, but that didn't mean they weren't part of the pride. They were, and they made a point of coming to every party they could. They wanted to see Teddy and the rest of the pride and spend time with them, something Teddy usually loved.

Not in this case.

"I'll find you a date," Nysys repeated. "Just tell me what kind of guy you like. Or girl?"

Teddy shook his head. There was no way he was having this conversation with Nysys. "I don't need to date."

"Sure you do. It's a party. Everyone needs a date."

"Even the teenagers? The kids?"

Nysys waved Teddy's words away. "You know what I mean. Come on. Tell me what you look for in a person."

Teddy didn't want to do this. He wouldn't allow Nysys to do it. "You don't need to find me a date. I already have one." The words were out before Teddy could think better of it. The only thing he wanted right now was to get rid of Nysys and go back to his books. He didn't want to fight over this. He didn't want to argue over it. He just wanted to be left in peace.

Nysys' eyes widened. "You really have a date? Have you been hiding a boyfriend?" He paused. "Or girlfriend?"

Teddy was pretty sure most of the house knew he was gay, but he didn't point it out. "Not a boyfriend. Just a guy."

Nysys' smile was blinding. "Well, the important thing is that you have someone. I'm happy for you, Teddy, and I hope it goes somewhere. And I'll be waiting to meet him. I can't wait."

Teddy almost groaned. What had he gotten himself into?

"Pass me the tool," Ollie said. He waved at the tool he needed and waited for Cyn to hand it to him.

Cyn arched a brow. "You mean the torque wrench?"

Ollie forced himself not to smile. "Yeah, that's what I meant."

Cyn passed it to him, then asked, "You're testing me?"

"I kind of have to if I want to hire you."

"You don't trust me."

It was more complicated than that. Ollie wanted to trust Cyn. Cyn was his best friend's mate, and that meant he wasn't going anywhere. Whatever happened, Cyn would be part of Ollie's life for years, decades. There was no way Ollie was moving away or abandoning Gabriel, so he had to make do with this guy.

Not that he didn't like Cyn. He didn't know him, and after the mess that had happened with Alice, he wasn't quite sure what to think of him. He wanted Gabriel to be happy, of course. If that meant that Gabriel needed to be with his mate, then so be it. Ollie would eventually get used to them as a couple, but it was hard not to be Ollie and Gabriel against the world anymore.

Gabriel didn't have as much time for Ollie as he had before. Ollie had expected it, but he couldn't help but feel slightly jealous. He knew that getting used to having Cyn in his life and welcoming him would change that. Time would, too. Right now, Cyn and Gabriel were just starting their relationship. They were still in the honeymoon phase, and it would probably last for a while. That meant Ollie spent more time alone than he was used to, and that made him crabby. He knew it wasn't his fault, but he didn't like it.

Of course Gabriel wanted to spend time with his mate. After everything they'd been through, Ollie didn't berate them for it. And after what Alice had done, they deserved not to have a second friend look down on their relationship. Ollie would never do that to Gabriel. But he couldn't deny he felt weird.

That was his problem, though. It didn't have anything to do with Gabriel or Cyn, and Ollie wasn't about to talk to Gabriel about it.

"It's not that I don't trust you," he began. He wasn't sure how to finish that, though.

Cyn leaned against the wall. He wore old clothes, just like Ollie, and it wasn't what Ollie had expected, knowing his past. He'd expected Cyn to come to work wearing designer clothes or something. He knew Cyn's parents were wealthy, and even though he didn't live with them anymore, it didn't mean the contents of his closet had changed.

But apparently, Cyn was serious about wanting to work with Ollie in the shop. He'd worn clothes that could get dirty and be thrown away without a problem, and that had been the first step toward Ollie's feelings toward him going the right way. Now all he needed to do was to make sure Cyn knew what he was doing with the bikes. He also needed to make sure Cyn wouldn't hurt Gabriel, but he wasn't quite sure how to do that.

Ollie wasn't the kind of guy who had *the talk* with Gabriel's boyfriends. He wasn't Gabriel's father. He wasn't even Gabriel's brother. They might have spent their teenage years together with the same foster family, but they weren't related. But they'd been best friends since they were teenagers, and that meant something. It didn't give Ollie an excuse to threaten Cyn, though, and he wouldn't do it. Gabriel was an adult, and he knew what he was doing. It was obvious that eventually, Cyn would hurt him, and he would hurt Cyn. Ollie would have to stay out of the situation because it would have nothing to do with him, so he might as well start now.

"It's that you don't know me. That I'm your best friend's mate, and you want to protect him," Cyn finished for Ollie.

Ollie had to nod. "Pretty much. I want to like you."

"Then do. It's not hard."

"It's not hard?"

"I like you. I like that you're Gabriel's friend and that I know he'll always have someone on his side."

Ollie couldn't help but grin at Cyn, who grinned back. "Now you're just buttering me up because you want this job."

Cyn laughed. "You're right. I want this job. Very much so. I love bikes." He ran a hand along one of the bikes Ollie needed to work on.

And Ollie needed help. He'd opened this shop a few years ago, and only thanks to the pack. Kameron had given him the money he needed, and he was still paying the alpha back. He would for several years, but things were starting to pick up, and on his own, he couldn't take all the jobs that walked through the door. If Cyn really knew his way around a bike, then Ollie wouldn't say no to hiring him.

"I don't know you. You're Gabriel's mate, though, and that means you're not going anywhere," Ollie said.

"I'm not. No matter what Alice wants."

Ollie grimaced. "I hate the way she behaved with you, but you have to understand."

"I do. I can't say I'm not still angry with her, or that I forgave her, but I do get where she's coming from. I don't have to like it, though."

Ollie knew that. Gabriel hadn't forgiven Alice yet. She was trying hard to accept that Cyn and Gabriel were an item and that Cyn wasn't going anywhere, but there was no denying how she'd behaved when Cyn had barged into Gabriel's life.

Gabriel was still pissed, but it would pass, eventually. He loved Alice like a sister. Both he and Ollie did.

The three of them had grown up together, and that meant a lot. There had been another two people in their small group, Lilah and Maddox. Lilah had left a long time ago, though, while Maddox had always been the quiet one. He'd never quite become a part of their group, and that meant that Ollie, Gabriel, and Alice had been like siblings. They'd done everything together, up until they moved out of the foster home.

Then Ollie had gone his own way. Gabriel and Alice had a back story they didn't share with him, and they'd stuck together. Now, Ollie couldn't help but wonder what would have happened if Gabriel had given himself a chance, if he'd maybe left for college. But instead, he'd decided he was in charge of Alice, and that he needed to help her, even if it meant putting himself second, and that was what he'd done.

But things were different now. Gabriel had met Cyn, and he'd realized that he and Alice couldn't be an island against the world. Alice was an adult just as much as Gabriel and Ollie, and she needed to take charge of her own life.

And she was. It wasn't easy, and Ollie could only imagine how bad she felt about the way Gabriel gave her the cold shoulder, but that was her own fault. He wouldn't be behaving this way if she hadn't treated Cyn the way she had.

"Guys?" Gabriel's voice asked from the tiny waiting room at the entrance of the building.

Cyn's expression lit up, and that was enough to tell Ollie how much Cyn cared for Gabriel.

He might not be sure about the guy yet, but he couldn't deny that Cyn cared for Gabriel, and that was all that mattered, wasn't it?

"Gabriel?" Cyn called back.

Gabriel appeared at the door, holding two plastic bags. He raised them and beamed at Cyn.

Ollie made a fake gagging sound. "You two are so fucking sweet. You're going to give me diabetes."

Gabriel scowled at him for a second. "That's not how it works."

Ollie didn't point out that he already knew that. Gabriel had mentioned it a few times because this was Ollie's recurring joke when he was with Cyn and Gabriel. He couldn't help it, though. Those two together were so sweet they would rot his teeth, and he was jealous.

He knew he was young, but so were Cyn and Gabriel. Yet they'd met each other and had fallen in love, and they were starting a life together. They weren't rushing into things, but they were dating, and they were happy.

Ollie wanted that, too. He wanted to have someone to text and call when he felt like it. He wanted someone to come home to every evening eventually. He wanted someone who would share his life, happiness and sorrow, all of it.

He could get a boyfriend or a girlfriend. It wasn't like he was always single or like he was waiting for his mate and that no one else would do.

But how was he supposed to be serious with someone when the possibility of meeting his mate was always there? That was something Ollie had always wondered, and he still didn't have an answer. He didn't know how other shifters did it, but he wasn't sure he could.

Would he be able to choose one of them if that was what it came to? Who, though? The person he loved, or the person he was supposed to love?

Those questions plagued his nightmares these days, maybe because of Cyn and Gabriel. But Ollie didn't want to think about that right now. He never wanted to think about it again. If and when he met his mate, he'd face the situation and make decisions. It was useless to think about this now. Hell, maybe he'd never meet his mate.

But part of him really hoped he would meet his other half the way Gabriel had. He wanted that happiness, that shared life only mated couples could have.

"Teddy has a boyfriend," Nysys announced when he and Teddy walked into the kitchen.

Everyone turned to look at them. Teddy's first instinct was to run away, but he stood his ground. It was mostly because he didn't think anyone would let him get away with hiding in his bedroom, though. If he'd been sure no one would follow him, he would have left right away.

"Did you really have to announce it that way?" he asked Nysys.

Nysys looked unrepentant. "Why not? Everyone's been wondering whether or not you would ever get a boyfriend."

"I told you he's not a boyfriend. He's just some guy I'm talking with."

Nysys put his hands on his hips. "You said he would be your date to the party."

"If he can, yes." Of course, Teddy wouldn't have a date for the party. He wouldn't have a date because he didn't have a boyfriend or any guy he was talking to. He didn't even have friends outside the pride. He was always too focused on books and school. He didn't have time to have friends.

And he was panicking. He knew Nysys well enough to be aware that the Nix wouldn't take no for an answer. Now that Teddy had told him he had a date, Nysys would expect to meet that date. If he didn't, he wouldn't hesitate to find a boyfriend for Teddy, and that was the last thing Teddy wanted.

He was fine on his own. He didn't need a guy, especially not when he didn't have time for one. He would have all the time in the world once he's finished his degree.

Well, maybe not. Once he was done with grad school, he

would have to find a job, and it would take him a few years to start his own firm. But as soon as he was done with that, he would have time to date. But not before. He couldn't allow himself to care for anyone when he didn't have time for them. It wouldn't be fair.

Nysys dropped his hands and headed toward the fridge. "Who is this guy, anyway? You've never talked about him."

Teddy rubbed his face. He needed to find a way out of this situation. He didn't have a guy to introduce to Nysys and the rest of the pride. "Just a guy from somewhere."

Nysys frowned. "Somewhere? That doesn't tell me anything. You met him in school? Or maybe in town?"

"He's from Gillham," someone said.

Teddy's heart raced. What was Sterling talking about? What was he doing?

Nysys blinked and turned to look at Sterling. "What are you doing here, anyway?"

Sterling arched a brow. "Are you saying you're not happy to see me?"

"Of course I'm happy to see you. I just thought you should move in with Adam, not the other way around."

Sterling grimaced. "You know why I didn't."

Because Sterling's parents had died, and he and Adam were raising his siblings. Everyone here knew it, and Teddy was satisfied to see the smile on Nysys' face falling. "Right. Sorry about that. But what were you saying about Teddy's boyfriend?"

Sterling's gaze collided with Teddy's. Teddy knew he probably looked panicked, but he didn't know what to do about it. He had no idea what Sterling was talking about or why he was doing this. He couldn't even remember the last time he'd been to Gillham, let alone when he'd met someone from there except for Sterling. "I said that I know Teddy's boyfriend. He's from Gillham. That's probably why you haven't seen him around a lot."

Nysys snorted, grabbed a bottle of water from the fridge, and closed it. "A lot? You mean that I haven't seen him at all, right? Because Teddy has been keeping this a secret, and I don't like secrets."

Teddy pinched the bridge of his nose. He didn't know what to do. He wanted to tell Sterling to shut up and not give Nysys more ideas, but Sterling might be saving his ass right now, and that was exactly what he needed.

"Come on, give me more details," Nysys said. He pointed his thumb at Teddy. "This one won't tell me anything, not even the guy's name."

Sterling raised his hands. "I'm not going to give you any details Teddy doesn't want you to have. If you want to meet this guy, I'm sure he'll be at the party. That's what you were talking about, isn't it?"

Nysys' expression lit up again. "Yes! That's exactly what I was talking about. I wanted to find Teddy a date, then he told me he already had one, and now I can't wait."

"Aren't you more excited about your mate's birthday party than about meeting my date?" Teddy asked. He knew better than to try to distract Nysys. That never worked, not for long, anyway.

Nysys shrugged. "As you said, Morin will have more than enough birthday parties in the future. But when will I ever have the occasion to meet your date for the first time?"

Teddy looked down. "I don't even know if we'll date or not. I told you, there's nothing serious between us."

"It's serious enough that you're seeing the guy. I'm pretty sure he's your first boyfriend, right?"

Teddy wanted to disappear. He wanted the earth to swallow him. "I had boyfriends in high school."

"You did? But you never brought anyone home."

That was because Teddy hadn't wanted to. In the first few

years after he'd moved in with the Jayden and Heath, he'd been trying to find a steadiness he'd missed most of this life. It hadn't been easy, and he'd been afraid the pride would kick him out for having a boyfriend. It was ridiculous considering more than half the people who lived with the pride were gay or in a same-sex relationship, but Teddy hadn't been able to help the way he felt.

He knew no one here would push him away. They wouldn't reject him. He was part of the family, and that would never change. That didn't mean he wanted Nysys and Keenan or anyone else to stick their noses into his private life, though. That was what he wanted—a *private* life. It was almost impossible to have when you lived with the pride, but he was working hard on it. Of course, the fact that he didn't actually have one helped.

"It's because it was nothing serious," he told Nysys. "None of my relationships were. I didn't bother to bring them here because they didn't matter, not in the long run. And this one might not either, so don't get your hopes up."

"As long as I see you with your date at the party, I'll be happy," Nysys said.

Somehow, Teddy doubted that was true.

He strode to the fridge and grabbed a bottle of water, then headed back to the living room. "I have to finish the chapter I was reading. Sorry I can't help you," he yelled over his shoulder as he left the kitchen.

"That's not fair!" Nysys yelled back. "You need to stop studying for a while."

But Teddy had already taken a ten-minute break, and that was more than enough. He needed to get back to it, and the sooner, the better.

"Teddy, wait up," Sterling said. He and Adam followed Teddy out of the kitchen, and Teddy wasn't sure what to do. He wanted to ask Sterling what he'd been thinking, but also to thank him.

"Sorry about that," Sterling said as he and Adam reached Teddy.

Teddy looked around. He might not know what was going on or what would happen, but he didn't want Nysys to overhear this conversation. "Why did you tell him I had a boyfriend and that you know him?" he asked quietly.

Sterling grimaced. "I'm sorry. I shouldn't have, but it was obvious to me that you'd lied to him, and I wanted him to stop poking at you."

"Why would you think I lied to him?"

Teddy didn't like the pity on Sterling's face. "You don't even have friends, Teddy. How could you have a boyfriend? I mean, I'm not trying to be offensive, but I know that your life revolves around school. And that's okay. It's perfectly fine, and no one should have anything to say about that. It's your life, and you live it the way you want to. But it was obvious you needed a way out, and we both know Nysys would have found you a date if you had told him you didn't have anyone."

Teddy raked a hand through his hair. "But now I have to find one. Nysys will find me someone if I come to the party on my own, and if I'm alone, he's going to bug me. I don't want him to find out I lied."

"Then find a date for the party."

Teddy glared. "And who am I supposed to bring? You just said yourself that my only friends are my books."

Sterling grimaced. "I'm sorry about that. I didn't mean to be rude."

Teddy sighed heavily. "It's okay. Thank you for trying to help me." Maybe Teddy could tell Nysys his imaginary boyfriend had broken up with him or something.

"But I think I have the perfect fake boyfriend for you," Sterling continued.

Teddy blinked at him. "I'm sorry?"

"I have the perfect fake boyfriend for you. That's why I said that your boyfriend was from Gillham. I know Nysys knows a lot of people there, but not all of the pack members, and Ollie is one."

"Ollie?" Adam finally asked.

Sterling gestured. "You know, the bike guy."

Adam's eyes widened. "You think he would agree to play fake boyfriends for Teddy?"

"I don't see why not."

Teddy wanted to say no. He *should* say no. But he couldn't help but think about what would happen if he ever told Nysys he was lying, or if he showed up at the party on his own.

He *couldn't* say no. "You know this Ollie guy?"

Sterling smiled at him. "He's a friend, kind of."

"Tell him the truth," Adam said.

"Okay, the fact is, I don't think I've ever talked to him. He's older, and we don't have the same friends. But I've seen him around. He grew up with the pack since he was a teenager. He's a good guy. All of them are. But I know for sure that he's single, and that his best friend found his mate. I'm sure he feels lonely, too."

Teddy crossed his arms over his chest. "This isn't about being lonely."

"You're right. It's about you lying to your family. And I'm not berating you for that. Nysys can be pushy when he wants to, which is most of the time. But it's either this, or you tell him the truth."

Just the thought of doing that made Teddy want to throw up. "Okay, I'm listening. Tell me about Ollie."

The house was noisy, just like when Ollie had lived here. Most of them had been teenagers back then, but once they'd gotten used to living here and they'd accepted that Mary Jane and Bill wouldn't kick them out, this had become their home, and they hadn't kept the noise down. These kids weren't, either, and it put a smile on Ollie's face.

Mary Jane and Bill had been fostering kids for close to fifteen years now, and Ollie had been one of the first. They weren't his parents, but he considered them family. He'd been fifteen when he'd arrived in Gillham, and even though he was too old to have them adopt him, he didn't think about his birth parents as his family, not anymore, maybe not ever.

He closed the door. "I'm home!" he yelled.

He waited, smiling at the sound of people running down the stairs. They sounded like a small herd of elephants, but in reality, they were only three kids, ranging from ages eight to twelve. They almost fell on top of each other on their way to Ollie, and he opened his arms for them. They threw themselves at him, almost knocking him on his ass as he hugged them and laughed.

"Honestly, kids," Mary Jane said.

Ollie looked up to see her stepping into the entrance, drying her hands on a kitchen towel. "At least let him take his jacket off."

Ella, the oldest, looked at Mary Jane. "But we've missed him," she whined.

Mary Jane pointed at the downstairs bathroom. "I'm sure he missed you too, but it's almost time for dinner, and I need the three of you to wash your hands."

Ollie kissed the top of Christopher's head—he was the youngest at eight—and gently pushed him toward the bathroom. "Come on. You know better than making her wait."

Emily, the third kid, grimaced and rushed toward the bathroom, knowing the kind of punishment that would be doled out if they didn't obey.

It had been the same one when Ollie had lived here, even

though he'd been fifteen. Either you obeyed and ate all your food, or you didn't get dessert. It was horrible, since Mary Jane was a great baker and always baked something for dinner.

She opened her arms to him, and Ollie hugged her gently. She kissed his cheek, then stepped back. "They're right, you know? We've missed you."

Ollie forced himself to smile at her. He was happy to be here. He always was. But ever since lunch, he couldn't help but feel unsettled. He wasn't sure if it was because he'd seen Gabriel so happy with Cyn or because he was jealous.

He wanted Gabriel to be happy. He wanted himself to be happy, too, though, and he didn't know how to make that happen. He hoped that having dinner with his family would help, but he wasn't so sure anymore.

Mary Jane's eyes narrowed, and she reached up to pat Ollie's cheek. "What's going on in that head of yours, Ollie?"

Ollie shook his head. "I'm okay. Just feeling weird."

Mary Jane frowned. "You know you can talk to me."

"Of course I know." Even though she wasn't his mother and she had three sons of her own, she'd been more of a mom to him than his biological mother. Ollie knew his mom and saw her sometimes, even though he never really wanted to. But he couldn't help but feel guilty about going with no contact with her, especially since she wasn't around a lot. So he allowed her to stay in his life, even though he felt like shit every time he saw her.

But Mary Jane was different. She was his mother, even though he'd been fifteen when he'd met her, even though she had her own sons.

"You don't have to be ashamed, whatever is going on in that head of yours," Mary Jane said. "Trust me, I've heard it all."

Ollie knew she was telling the truth. She and her mate, Bill, had arrived in Gillham with her three sons after one of them had met his mate. Ollie had never found out the entire story, but it didn't matter. Mary Jane and Bill had been a part of the pack for more than fifteen years, and even more so when they'd started welcoming foster kids who didn't have another place to go.

"It's nothing, really," he said, feeling ridiculous. "I just spent half my day with Gabriel and his mate."

Mary Jane beamed. "I'm so happy he found his mate." Her smile fell a bit. "Aren't you?"

"Of course I'm happy for him. You have to know that."

She pursed her lips. "You know, sometimes, I couldn't help but wonder if there might have been something between you and Gabriel."

Ollie jerked back, grimacing. "Something? Please tell me it's not what I'm thinking of."

Mary Jane shrugged. "Why not? It's not like you're related."

"Maybe not, but he feels like a brother, and that's never going to change. No, I don't feel anything for him, not like that. I'm over the moon that he met his mate, even after everything that happened with Alice. That's not the problem here."

"Then what is it?"

Ollie didn't want to think about it anymore. He didn't want to talk about it. But he'd never been able to say no to Mary Jane. "I'm just jealous."

Mary Jane blinked. "But not of Gabriel's mate."

"No, not of him. As far as I know, he's a good guy. We spent the day together because he wants to work with me, and I think I'm going to hire him eventually."

"So what's the problem? What are you jealous of? Is it because Gabriel has someone else in his life now and doesn't have as much time for you anymore?"

"It's part of it. I won't deny that. But it's not my main problem with this. I know I'm a selfish asshole who should be happy for his brother, but I can't help but wonder when I'll meet my own mate, you know?"

Mary Jane's smile softened, became more understanding. "You're so young, Ollie."

"I know I'm young. I know I have all my life in front of me to find my mate, and I wasn't in a rush to find him. But I see Gabriel and Cyn together, and I want the same thing, you know? I want the type of relationship they have, and I've never found it with anyone."

"There's nothing to say you'll find it with your mate. You know that's not how it works."

It wasn't, but Ollie knew that being with his mate would give him a chance at it. Even though he'd had boyfriends and girlfriends, even though he'd loved some of them, it hadn't been the same. There hadn't been that deep understanding Gabriel and Cyn shared and Ollie yearned for.

And maybe that was wrong. Maybe that wasn't what a mate was meant to be. But that was what Ollie wanted. He wanted someone who would be there for him through everything. He wanted someone for whom he could be the center of the world.

He realized that probably stemmed from the way he'd been abandoned. He'd never known his father, at least not until he got the man's name out of his mother. And even after he'd found out, he'd never contacted him. He didn't want to. He already had a family. But he couldn't deny he'd been abandoned, first by his father, then by his mother, even though she came around sometimes. It didn't lessen the pain he'd felt at fifteen when he'd been forced to go with the foster family. He couldn't deny the pain of knowing that he wasn't important enough for her to make her stay with him instead of traveling around the world.

He was an adult now, but it still hurt sometimes, and it still influenced the way he viewed relationships. He wanted someone who would never abandon him, and his mate might be the perfect person for that. They were supposed to be perfect for him. They were supposed to want to be with him for the rest of their life. That was what bonding with your mate meant.

And Ollie wanted that. He wanted that so freaking much that sometimes, it was hard to breathe. He hadn't realized that until now. It had been easy to ignore this kind of feeling, but now, he was forced to confront it because of Gabriel and Cyn.

He had no idea what to do with himself or how to deal with the feelings.

Mary Jane patted Ollie's cheek again. "Don't think about it. I know it's hard, but you can do it. Obsessing over finding your mate won't help you find him or her. Whenever you need them the most, they'll come, and they'll be there for you."

Ollie hoped Mary Jane was right, but in the meantime, he needed to do what she said. He needed to forget about his mate and stop wondering who they were. He needed to focus on what he already had instead of on what he wanted.

CHAPTER TWO

It was a conspiracy. There was no other word for it.

Every time Teddy sat down to study, someone interrupted him. He'd told everyone to stay away. He'd locked his door. But that wasn't enough. It was never enough for Nysys, who'd shimmered into his bedroom even though he wasn't supposed to. "Just tell me who he is," he insisted.

Teddy turned his chair around and glared at the Nix. "What are you even doing here? The door is locked."

Nysys shrugged. "I wanted to talk to you."

"Aren't you busy organizing the party?"

"I'm taking a break. Which you should do, too."

He'd been on Teddy's back to take a break for the past few days, ever since Teddy had lied to him and told him that he had a boyfriend, or rather, that he had a date for the party. The party was fast approaching, and Teddy had thought he'd have the next few days to study in peace, but he should have known better. Nysys was curious, and he'd been hounding him for a name.

Teddy hadn't heard from Sterling and Adam yet. He wasn't about to give Nysys a name, not when he wasn't sure their friend would do this for him. He still didn't think it was a good idea, but it was better than having to admit he'd lied and watching the pity and confusion and pain on Nysys' face. Teddy might have been wrong to lie to him, but he'd been pushed to it. This wasn't his fault. But even though Teddy knew that, he couldn't help but feel guilty. He didn't like to lie to anyone, not even Nysys, not even when he deserved it.

He had to find a way around this, but he wasn't sure how or what.

"I told Jayden."

Teddy's brain froze. "You did *what*?"

"I told Jayden you were bringing a date." Nysys crossed his arms over his chest and glared back at Teddy. "Why? Was it a secret?"

"Of course not." But Teddy had hoped this wouldn't happen. He'd hoped, well, he wasn't sure what he'd hoped.

He didn't want to lie to his brother. He hated lying to Nysys or to anyone, but Jayden was different. He was Teddy's brother, the one person who'd always been there for him, even when he wasn't physically present. Teddy didn't like the thought of not telling him the truth, but he wasn't sure he had a way out of this right now.

He could tell Nysys his fake boyfriend couldn't come to the party. He could tell Nysys that Ollie, Sterling and Adam's friend, had other things to do. What would Nysys do? It wasn't like he could find Teddy a boyfriend when he knew Teddy already had someone in his life, even if that person wasn't coming.

But Teddy wouldn't put it past Nysys to go find Ollie and ask him why he wasn't coming. If Nysys did that, all the lies would crumble, and Teddy couldn't deal with that. He shouldn't have lied in the first place, and now he was stuck. He didn't know how to get out of this, but he would have to find a way.

He rubbed his face. "What did he say?"

Nysys shrugged. "I think he was hurt you didn't tell him about it."

"I wasn't going to tell anyone. The only reason I told you about Ollie is that I knew you wouldn't leave me alone if I didn't."

Nysys' eyes widened. "Ollie?"

Shit. Teddy shouldn't have told Nysys Ollie's name. "Never mind. Just tell me about Jayden."

He could see the Nysys wanted to push, but he was relieved when he didn't. "I guess I thought he knew. I mean, he's your brother, and I know you two talk."

"Yeah, we do. But I haven't told anyone because what's between me and my date is so new. I don't even know if it's going to still be a thing by the time the party comes around."

"Of course it will be. I don't see why someone would dump you. You're cute, in a geekish, twinkish kind of way."

Teddy glared. "Can't you be nice for one second?"

"It was a compliment. I mean, I'm a twink, too. I'm not a geek, but I'm sure some people like that."

Teddy pinched the bridge of his nose. "All right. Just go, please. I need to study."

"Fine, I'm going, but not because you want to be alone. I'm going because I think Jayden is here, and he probably wants to talk to you."

Teddy snapped his head toward Nysys, but it was too late. For once, the Nix had obeyed and had shimmered out. Of course, that left Teddy panicking. Was Jayden really here? Did he think Teddy had a boyfriend he hadn't told him about?

A knock on the door told Teddy everything he needed to know. Yes, his brother was in the house, and he wanted to talk to him.

Teddy wanted to hide, but instead, he got up and unlocked the door. Sure enough, Jayden was standing on the other side of it, a frown on his face. Teddy opened his mouth to say something, even though he wasn't sure what, but Jayden got the first word in. "Why didn't you tell me?" he asked, stepping into the bedroom.

Teddy closed the door behind him. "Jayden—"

Jayden pulled on his hair. "I mean, I thought we were friends. If anything, we're brothers. You should have told me you had a boyfriend. Why didn't you?"

Teddy knew Jayden would start rambling if he didn't stop him in his tracks. "I don't have a boyfriend, not as such. It's just someone I'm seeing. There's nothing official between us, and I wouldn't even have told Nysys if he hadn't pushed for me to have a date for his stupid party. You know what he would have done if I'd told him I didn't have anyone. I didn't want to come to the party only to find out he'd arranged a date with someone in town."

Jayden didn't look convinced. "Are you sure?"

"If I'm sure I don't have a boyfriend? Yeah, I am." Teddy hated lying to his brother, and he was, kinda. It was true he didn't have a boyfriend, but hopefully, he'd have a date for the party and Jayden was hurt he didn't know about Teddy's maybe fake boyfriend. Jayden was one person Teddy didn't want to lie to, but he wasn't sure what else to do.

He knew Jayden wouldn't tell Nysys if Teddy admitted he didn't actually have anyone. But he might be even more disappointed than he was right now, and that wasn't something Teddy was ready to face. After everything Jayden had done for him, he wanted his brother to trust him.

Of course, he should probably stop lying for that to happen, but he couldn't, not in this case. It wasn't like he was lying about something important, anyway. Sure, he was telling people he had a guy in his life. It wasn't a big lie, though. He could tell Nysys and Jayden that Ollie had broken up with him before the party or something. It was probably the best thing to do, and that way, Jayden wouldn't be hurt by Teddy's lies. He might be disappointed because he thought Teddy should be more open to relationships, both with guys and with people in general, but he'd always known Teddy was a bit of a loner. It was in his DNA, in the way he'd been raised for the first thirteen years of his life. It was in what had happened to their mother.

Jayden might have managed to get over it, to find his mate and be happy, but Teddy was still trying to find his way through that, and that wouldn't change only because he had a boyfriend.

"I'll tell you if I ever have a boyfriend," Teddy told his brother. "I promise. The only reason I didn't this time was that, like I just said, we're not actually together. We've been talking, and yes, I like him. But that doesn't mean we're going to end up together. I'm not even sure he'll want to come to the party, especially when I let him know that Nysys told the entire pride we're together. I don't think he sees me as a boyfriend, but if he does, he hasn't told me, and I'm not going to assume. You know I'm not the best when it comes to this kind of social stuff."

Jayden's expression softened. "I think you sell yourself short. You would be great at relationships if you gave yourself a chance, but you're always so focused on school."

That wasn't something Teddy wanted to talk about. He already had people telling him he should take breaks almost every day, sometimes more than once a day. Nysys was still poking at him for that, and it was more than enough. "I'm just trying to finish my degree. Once that's done, I'll be able to relax." Teddy swallowed. "I want you to be happy for me. I want you to be proud of me."

"Of course I'm proud of you. I would never have imagined you'd be at this point in your life, but you are, and I *am* proud. But I don't think you should neglect your personal life for your professional one. That's all. No matter how happy you are studying, and later, working, your life can't revolve around that. You need people in your life, people who love you, and it won't help to push everyone away because they care."

"I'm not pushing anyone away. I just want some peace."

Jayden nodded. "I get it. But I hope you know I'm here for

you, whatever you need. You're my brother, and that's never going to change."

Teddy prayed that was the truth. He didn't know what Jayden would do if he found out Teddy had lied to him, but hopefully, since the lie was a small one, he wouldn't care.

Ollie couldn't help but smile. It had been a while since he and Gabriel had had an evening to themselves, and being here with his friend made something settle in Ollie's chest.

He clinked his beer bottle against Gabriel's and smiled at him. Gabriel smiled back, and everything was like it was before. Ollie knew it wouldn't last, but that was okay. He wanted Gabriel to be happy with Cyn and to go back home to him if that was what he wanted. But he also wanted to take advantage of this moment and be with his best friend.

"How are things going with Alice?" he asked. He almost regretted it right away when Gabriel grimaced, but he knew he had to ask.

He'd tried talking to Alice, but she'd closed herself off after what had happened. Ollie understood it and hadn't pushed, but eventually, Alice would have to talk to someone. He hoped that someone would be him, or even better, Gabriel, but it wasn't like he could choose for her.

Gabriel shrugged. "Things have been better. I won't lie. I'm still angry at her for what she did."

"That's understandable, but she's trying, right? Cyn mentioned something about that."

"She is. She hasn't been rude to him in a while, and she's making an effort. But I can't help but feel hurt when I look at her, you know? I know why she did it, and I know she regrets it, but it doesn't cancel the fact that she treated my mate like garbage or the fact that I almost lost him because of that. If she'd told me he'd come to the house sooner, we wouldn't have arrived just before he got married."

Ollie grimaced. "You think he would have said yes?"

"Of course not. His parents would have had to drag him to the altar kicking and screaming. But that doesn't mean whoever was supposed to officiate the wedding wouldn't have ignored that. I wouldn't be surprised if the man or the woman would've turned a blind eye. You know how much money Cyn's parents have. I don't trust them not to try to buy everyone, including the officiant and everyone present at the wedding."

Having so much money was mind-boggling to Ollie, but he knew Gabriel was right. He reached out and patted his best friend's hand. "Well, you got there in time, and you got Cyn back. You shouldn't continue thinking about that." He hesitated. "Unless his parents are making trouble? Have they contacted him?"

Gabriel shook his head. "Not as far as I know. Cyn would have told me. And yes, I know you're right, and I generally try not to think about it. But it's hard sometimes, especially when Alice is around. I want to forgive her. I hate being so distant from her and feeling so angry, but I can't help it. Even though I know she regrets it, the way she behaved still hurts. I wanted her to be happy for me, just like you are, and instead, she did what she did."

"It's going to take time."

"Exactly."

Ollie got it, and he hoped Alice understood it, too. He knew she was probably desperate to have Gabriel forgive her, but it wasn't easy. No matter how many times she apologized and how she behaved right now, it didn't change the fact that instead of wanting Gabriel to be happy, she'd been aiming for her own happiness. She'd tried pushing Gabriel's mate away because she didn't like him, and because she didn't want to lose Gabriel.

"Excuse me?"

The interruption made both of them look up. Ollie frowned at the two men standing by the table, trying to place them. He knew he'd seen them around, but he wasn't sure who they were. The pack had grown a lot over the past couple of decades, and now, there were a lot of people who didn't mingle, mostly because of the age difference, and those guys were younger than Ollie and Gabriel by close to a decade.

One of them thrust his hand out. "I'm Sterling, and this is Adam, my mate."

The names sparked something in Ollie's brain. "Of course." Everyone knew Sterling after what had happened to his parents. That was probably why Ollie recognized him. He and his mate were raising Sterling's siblings after his parents had died, even the one who was sixteen. They were barely older, maybe twenty, if even that, and Ollie was impressed by the fact that Sterling hadn't run away screaming at the thought of those responsibilities.

He shook Sterling's hand. "I'm Ollie, and this is Gabriel."

Sterling smiled. "I was wondering if I could talk to you for a second?"

Ollie and Gabriel looked at each other. Neither of them knew what Sterling wanted, and Ollie was curious. Besides, he suspected Gabriel could do with a break in their conversation.

He gestured at the empty seats at the table. "Sit down."

Sterling and Adam obeyed. Sterling looked nervous, while Adam seemed amused. Ollie was curious to find out what they wanted more than ever, so he waited, giving Sterling time to gather his thoughts.

Sterling leaned forward. "I have a proposition for you. Well, more like a favor to ask you, actually."

Ollie blinked. "We don't know each other. What kind of favor would you need to ask from me?" Maybe he had a bike or something. Maybe he needed someone to fix it.

"I have a friend," Sterling continued. That wasn't going where Ollie had expected, but he nodded and waited for Sterling to continue.

Sterling did. "His name is Teddy, and he's a member of the Whitedell pride. He needs a fake boyfriend."

Ollie waited, convinced there was more to this situation, but when Sterling didn't continue and instead stared at him expectantly, Ollie had to ask, "Why does he need a fake boyfriend?"

Sterling rubbed the back of his neck. "You know I sometimes visit the pride. Adam is from there, and he likes spending time with his family. We were there the other day, and Nysys, one of the pride's members, is organizing a party. He's kind of pushy, and he wants everyone to be happy, so he wanted to find Teddy a boyfriend. He wants Teddy to have a date for this party, and he's not taking no for an answer."

"Okay. I know some people can be pushy, but I'm not sure where I come in. I mean, why are you telling *me* this?"

Gabriel snorted, but Ollie ignored him. He focused on Sterling instead because he wanted to understand.

"Teddy told Nysys he already had a date so Nysys wouldn't organize one for him. It wasn't a bad idea, because while Nysys always means well, more often than not, his plans take a bad turn. But Teddy is stuck now because the entire pride expects him to come to the party with a guy. Of course, since it was a lie, he doesn't *actually* have a boyfriend."

"Hence why he needs a fake one."

Sterling's eyes lit up. "Exactly. And you came to mind when I thought about this."

Ollie leaned back in his chair. "Why? You don't know me."

Sterling shrugged. "Not personally. But I've seen you around, and I know you've been a pack member for more than ten years. I know you're a good person. I also know you don't know anyone in Whitedell, so I thought it would be a good idea if you could be Teddy's fake boyfriend. No one in Whitedell will find that strange."

This could go wrong in so many ways that Ollie couldn't even think of all of them right now. But for whatever reason, he found himself wanting to say yes. He wanted to help Teddy, whoever Teddy was. Maybe this would distract him from the jealousy he felt every time he watched Gabriel and Cyn together.

He was happy for Gabriel, and even for Cyn, but now that he had more time to dwell on his thoughts, he found that he didn't want to be jealous. Maybe taking this *job* as a fake boyfriend for an evening would be fun and would help distract him. "What are the details?" he asked.

Sterling's eyes widened. "Does that mean you're saying yes?"

"It means I want to hear more about this. You need to tell me the situation I'd be walking into if I said yes. I won't confirm until I know what's going to happen, but I'm interested."

Sterling grinned. "Great. It goes like this—"

Teddy's phone chirped, but he ignored it and kept his focus on his textbook, or at least, he tried to.

He couldn't stop thinking about the conversation he and Jayden had had a few hours ago, though. He'd hurt Jayden, and that was the last thing he ever wanted to do. He owed so much to his brother, and they were a family. Teddy never wanted to lose that, and even though he knew that Jayden wouldn't kick him out of their family because he lied to him about it, he was still terrified.

The fear was making it hard to focus on his studies, so he finally put down his pen and leaned back in his chair. He rubbed his burning eyes and closed them, forcing his body to relax. He felt so tense that he might break if someone touched him, and he wasn't sure what to do about it.

Night had fallen, and Teddy had stayed in his bedroom. He hadn't even gone downstairs to get dinner because he'd wanted to avoid Nysys, and he wasn't hungry. He should probably eat something, though. He was too tired to do anything right now. He was still afraid he'd meet Nysys if he went downstairs, but maybe in a few hours. Nysys would go back home eventually, right?

Teddy didn't think he was up to studying anymore, not with how gritty his eyes felt. Maybe he could take a break, check his phone, then go downstairs to grab something to eat. He wasn't sure he'd be able to keep his eyes open long enough to study some more once he was done eating, but he would try. He always did.

He snagged his phone from the desk and checked the messages. The one on top was from a number he didn't recognize, and he frowned as he opened it.

There were two texts. The first one said, *hi. I'm Ollie.*

Teddy swallowed and scrolled down.

I know this is weird. I wasn't sure what to do when Sterling gave me your phone number, even though he explained what you need. It is weird, right?

Teddy chuckled. He wanted to answer, but he wasn't sure how. What was he supposed to say to this guy? He supposed Sterling had explained what Teddy needed, so Ollie didn't need more explanations. Teddy should introduce himself, but he didn't know how.

Another text arrived before he could make a decision. *So, Sterling explained what you need from me. Looks like I'm your boyfriend?*

Teddy couldn't help but smile. He quickly typed, *fake boyfriend.*

That got him a smiley face from Ollie.

Teddy was embarrassed. He wasn't quite sure how to deal

with Ollie. This was the first time they'd spoken, and Ollie had agreed to play Teddy's fake boyfriend. Teddy couldn't understand why Ollie had, but he wasn't about to try to change his mind.

Fake boyfriend, Ollie agreed in his next message. *I have to say I was kind of weirded out when Sterling told me about this. I mean, I don't think I've ever talked to him or his mate before tonight.*

Teddy closed his eyes and groaned. Sterling had warned him that he didn't actually know Ollie, and Teddy hadn't been sure he would go through with this. He'd thought that maybe Sterling would find someone else, someone he knew. Surely, Sterling had friends in the pack? But instead, he'd decided to talk to Ollie and make a fool out of Teddy. It was a miracle that Ollie was talking to Teddy rather than ignoring him.

I'm so sorry about that, Teddy answered.

Sorry about what?

About Sterling. He's right, I do need a fake boyfriend for a party, but I didn't expect him to talk to you.

Why don't you tell me what happened?

I thought Sterling already had?

He mentioned a few things, but I want to hear it from you.

Teddy rose from his chair and flopped onto his bed. His back hurt from being in the same position for so long, and he rolled his head over his shoulders as he thought of what to write.

Things went like this – one of the pride members is organizing a party for his mate.

A birthday party? Ollie asked.

Exactly. So he's organizing this party, and he asked me if I was bringing a date.

And you're not.

Nope. I also wasn't planning to find one. I'm still in school, and I'm focusing on my studies. I don't have time for boyfriends or a relationship.

Understandable.

Teddy smiled at that answer. Sometimes, he thought no one understood why he was behaving the way he was. Most people didn't realize that he owed so much to his brother that he needed to do well at school, but even those who did weren't sure why he was so focused on this. They couldn't understand, and Teddy wasn't about to explain. This was his problem, not theirs. Still, sometimes, he wished people would stop bugging him.

And since I knew that Nysys would find me someone if I didn't show up with a date, I lied to him.

Why would he do that?

Teddy's smile widened. It was refreshing to speak to someone who didn't know Nysys. *Because he sticks his nose into everyone's business. He's a sweet guy, and I know he only wants me to be happy. He wants everyone to be as happy as he is. But he's still nosy and impulsive. If I hadn't told him I already had a date, he would have found someone for me, and I can't be sure it would have been someone I'll like. So when he said he would find me a date, I told him I already had one. That's where the problems started.*

Teddy's phone vibrated with the answer. *Problems?*

Well, now he wants to meet my boyfriend.

Your date.

You're right, my date. I did tell him that I'm not boyfriends with this guy and that I'm just talking to him, things like that. I warned him this wasn't serious. I thought that would be enough to keep him away, but I should have known better. Now he expects to see me with my date at the party, and I'm not sure what to do.

You find yourself a boyfriend, Ollie answered.

Teddy realized he'd been smiling since the first message. He'd thought things would be awkward between him and Ollie, considering what Teddy was asking of him and the fact that they didn't know each other, but they weren't. It felt good to be able to talk to someone who didn't know him and who wouldn't judge him. Ollie didn't actually care about Teddy.

He didn't want Teddy to be happy. He didn't want Teddy to find love, or whatever else Nysys wanted everyone to find. He was just curious and asking questions.

I wasn't sure what to say when Nysys said he expected to meet my boyfriend at the party. I kind of froze, but then Sterling said he knew my boyfriend, Teddy typed.

So he put both of us in trouble.

I don't know if I would call this trouble, not for you. I mean, you don't actually have to say yes. I was relieved when Sterling stepped in because I didn't know what to tell Nysys, but I won't deny it was terrifying when he said he knew my boyfriend and I had no idea who he was talking about. Luckily, he didn't give Nysys a name.

Teddy had, though. He wasn't sure what he would do if Ollie backed out of this. It wasn't like he could find another guy with the same name who would agree to do this for him.

I'm not backing out of this, don't worry. I need a distraction, Ollie texted, as if reading Teddy's thoughts.

Teddy's shoulders slumped in relief. *Thank you. I'm not sure what I'll do if I don't have you by my side at the party.*

But he'd already decided that if Ollie couldn't do this, if he wasn't willing to help, he'd show up on his own and tell Nysys they'd broken up. Nysys would pout and mope, but he'd be focused on his mate and knowing that Teddy might be heartbroken, he would probably give him the benefit of the doubt and a few days to wrap his mind around his break-up.

Whatever happened, whatever Ollie decided, Teddy would be okay. He'd find a way out of this, and he'd go back to his studies.

Ollie was curious about Teddy, so while he texted him on his phone, he dragged his laptop closer and opened the browser. Sterling had given him Teddy's name and his phone number, and Ollie used them to find Teddy on social media. There wasn't much to see, much less than Ollie expected, and he was surprised. Although maybe he shouldn't have been, considering what he'd been told about Teddy. It wasn't much, but Sterling had explained that Teddy was focused on school and that he didn't have much time for anything else. What Teddy had said confirmed that, so Ollie wasn't surprised to see that Teddy's profile was almost empty. There were a few pictures, though, and Teddy looked adorable in them.

Teddy was exactly what Ollie thought of as a geek, a nerd. He was cute, on the smaller side, and thin. In the picture Ollie was looking at, he was wearing a t-shirt from some kind of movie, or at least Ollie thought so. He also had glasses, and it looked like they might slip off his nose at any second. Teddy's hair was all over the place, and rather than smiling, he was scowling as if someone had taken it without his knowledge. That couldn't be right, since Teddy had uploaded it, but it made Ollie even more curious.

What kind of guy was Teddy? The only thing Ollie knew about him was that he studied a lot, but that wasn't much. He wanted to know more.

He clicked through Teddy's friends, and all of them were based in Whitedell. He found one with the name Teddy kept bringing up—Nysys—and clicked over to the man's profile.

Nysys was incredibly different from Teddy. Where Teddy's hair was a normal color, Nysys had bright pink hair and a lot of tattoos. A lot of piercings, too. Ollie liked all those things on a guy, but he could have done without the pink hair. Nysys was cute, though, and also very much mated, from the pictures Ollie could see.

He quickly ran through Nysys' public profile, smiling at the fact that he seemed to be posting pictures of weird sex toys on pretty much anyone's profile, including Teddy's.

Ollie went back to Teddy's profile. He looked at the picture again, cocking his head this way and that, trying to read the man he was supposed to be dating.

So Teddy was kind of a nerd. That shouldn't be as adorable as it was, and Ollie wasn't about to tell Teddy that. Still, he couldn't deny it was part of Teddy's charm. Teddy looked like the kind of guy who didn't know he was cute, or maybe who didn't care. Ollie wouldn't be surprised if that was the case.

He turned back to his phone. *So, how did we meet? We should probably come up with a story*, he texted.

He was having fun, much more than he expected.

He hadn't been sure what to think when Sterling and Adam approached him, but he was glad he'd listened to their story. He didn't know Teddy, but he was looking forward to meeting him. He wanted to help him. He understood the expectations people had, and he understood why Teddy didn't want to meet them. He was doing his own thing, focusing on school, and that was good. Ollie had never gone to college, but when he worked on the bikes in his shop, he forgot about everything else. So he got it.

He also understood why Teddy didn't want people to think he didn't have a boyfriend, though. Nysys seemed like a quirky guy from his social media presence, and Teddy texted as if he cared for the guy, but it looked like Nysys might be overbearing — trying to do the right thing, but pushing too much. It was almost as if he didn't understand why Teddy didn't care about boyfriends, and he only wanted to help Teddy the only way he knew. If Teddy didn't want to disappoint his family or to have Nysys hounding him to get a guy, he needed to find a way to get Nysys off his back.

I suck at inventing stories, Teddy texted back.

What are you studying? Not English literature?

Ollie could almost hear the snort coming with Teddy's answer. *No, not English literature. I'm working on a Master's degree in accounting. How should we say we met, then?*

Ollie tapped his fingertips on his thigh. *What do you think? Maybe we should stick to the truth as much as possible. We could* tell people we met through Sterling and Adam. I didn't know them before, but I knew of them. It wouldn't take much to tweak this and make them my friends, and since Sterling knows you, he could have introduced us. He actually did, so that wouldn't be a lie.

That sounds good. I hate lying, so the less we can do it, the better I will feel.

Ollie smiled. He liked Teddy already, even though they barely knew each other. *I get that. So they introduced us, and we started texting. That's the truth, too. Since you told Nysys that we weren't boyfriends yet, we can say that we just limited ourselves to text back and forth. You sound very busy, and I own a motorcycle shop, so it's plausible. You don't have to tell him that the party will be the first time we meet since Sterling and Adam are supposed to have introduced us, but it could be the second one.*

The three dots that told Ollie that Teddy was typing back blinked onto the screen, disappeared, then came back. Ollie realized he was holding his breath, waiting for Teddy's answer, and he wasn't sure why.

Sure, he felt better about agreeing to do this. He realized that Teddy really needed his help, and it was nice to feel needed. He'd been worried he was doing the wrong thing, but he knew he wasn't, not anymore. He wanted to help Teddy in this little white lie, but he also wanted to see more of Teddy.

Ollie was surprised. He'd had plenty of people in his life, boyfriends and girlfriends who came and went, but no one important. He didn't usually get curious about people without ever meeting them, though. Teddy was the first, and Ollie couldn't wait to find out more about him.

Do you think they'll believe us if we say this is only the second time we've met? Teddy finally answered.

Ollie wrinkled his nose at how long it had taken Teddy to type that. *Why would they care? Again, you told them we weren't a couple yet. It would make sense that we only met once and texted for the rest, considering how busy we both are. There's also the fact that you're in Whitedell, and I'm in Gillham. That adds to how plausible the situation is. We can come up with another story, though, if you want.*

No, it's fine. I just hate lying, you know? Nysys told my brother I had a boyfriend, and Jayden was so disappointed I hadn't told him.

Ollie grimaced. *I understand that. Brothers are great to have, but sometimes, you want to keep some things from them.* Like how jealous Ollie was of Gabriel's relationship with Cyn. He didn't want to tell Gabriel about that because Gabriel deserved to be able to focus on his mate and their relationship. He knew Gabriel was slightly worried, though. Hopefully, their evening together had soothed his worry.

You have brothers? Teddy asked.

Foster brothers, yes. The one I'm closest to is Gabriel, and he just found his mate. I'm over the moon for him, but also a bit jealous.

It took a moment for Teddy to answer. *You want to meet your mate?*

Ollie blinked. *Don't you?*

Like I told you before, I need to focus on my studies. I don't have time for a relationship, and that would be even worse with a mate.

Ollie frowned. *You wouldn't kick him to the curb, right?*

Again, it took Teddy a moment to answer, and Ollie held his breath until the text appeared on his phone. *I wouldn't kick him to the curb, no. I wouldn't even reject him, I don't think. Honestly, I haven't thought about it. I haven't thought about guys because I don't have time for them.*

But this wouldn't be just a boy. It would be your mate.

That's why I would give him a chance, but he would have to understand that school will always come first for me. I need to do well. I can't get distracted.

As long as you give him a chance, I think you'll be okay. Or at least, Ollie hoped so.

Teddy sounded like a good guy. A bit weird, maybe, but who wasn't weird in some ways? But he was focused on school, and that probably wasn't going to change until he finished his degree. Ollie could only imagine he would put this focus into finding a job, too, and he kind of felt sorry for the guy's mate if they met before Teddy was settled in his life.

That wasn't his business, though, was it?

CHAPTER THREE

Teddy looked at himself in the mirror. Was this good enough? Or would Nysys have something to say about the way he was dressed?

He didn't do parties. He was always too busy studying, and even when he was invited, he tended to avoid them or go for only a few minutes. He knew Nysys wouldn't accept that, though. He'd want to see Teddy, especially since Teddy had told him his date was coming.

Teddy closed his eyes and sighed. Maybe this was a bad idea. Maybe he should text Ollie and tell him he'd changed his mind and that he didn't want Ollie to come. That would probably be best for everyone involved, including Teddy.

He was a liar. He didn't like being a liar.

He and Ollie had texted, and he liked the guy. He was fun, and he hadn't said anything about the way Teddy was behaving. He hadn't pointed out that Teddy was lying to his family, and Teddy was grateful for that. But he knew that the situation could end badly.

What had he been thinking?

Teddy stepped away from the mirror and pulled on his hair—or at least he tried to, but it was frozen in place by the gel he'd had to use to tame it. He needed to find a way out of this, and he wasn't sure there was one. The party was already going strong downstairs, but he was hiding in his bedroom. That wouldn't be allowed for long, though. Nysys would realize eventually, and he'd come after Teddy and drag him downstairs kicking and screaming if that was what it took.

But Teddy wasn't ready. Of course, he doubted he'd ever be ready to face the situation.

A knock on the door made him jump. He looked at it, panic growing in his chest. "Yes?" he called out.

"What are you doing in there?" Nysys answered.

Of course it was him. Teddy had expected it, but now that he was confronted with the reality of what he'd done, he wasn't sure what to do. "I'm almost ready."

There was a pause before Nysys answered, "Almost ready? You're saying that as if you're putting more care into your appearance than usual."

Teddy rubbed the back of his neck, searching for something to say. "Well, I have a date tonight. It's obvious I'm putting more effort into the way I look."

"Attaboy. Okay, I'll be back in five minutes. You better be ready by then. You've already missed the first hour of the party, and we're having so much fun."

Teddy listened to him walking away, then sighed and flopped onto his bed.

He was wearing jeans and a t-shirt, nothing incredible, and Nysys would probably wrinkle his nose in that disapproving way of his when he saw him. If Teddy knew him well—and he did—Nysys was no doubt wearing some kind of outrageous clothing, colorful and tight, something that Teddy would never wear himself.

Teddy was kind of boring, and he tended to stick to jeans and t-shirts. Today wasn't any different, even though he couldn't deny he'd made an effort with his hair. The curly mess was usually hell to deal with, and today hadn't been any different, but with the help of a lot of gel, it should stay in place. Of course, it also felt stiff and unmoving, and Teddy didn't like it, but it wasn't like he had any other choice.

Actually, he did. He wasn't sure why he'd done his hair. The party was at home, and most of the people who would be there were people who lived with the pride. None of them would care if he came downstairs in his pajamas, except maybe Nysys — and Ollie. But Ollie didn't have to be there. Teddy still had time to text him and tell him not to come.

Which was why Teddy reached for his phone. He opened the string of texts he and Ollie had been exchanging since Ollie had texted him the first time. He quickly scrolled up, reading a few of them and smiling as he did so. Ollie was a nice guy, and Teddy almost wished they really were dating. The fact that he didn't have time for a boyfriend didn't seem to matter, not when it came to Ollie. He was a tempting man, and Teddy hadn't even met him face to face yet. He was almost scared to find out what would happen when he did.

But he couldn't. He couldn't allow this to happen. Asking Ollie to come to the party had been a bad idea, and Teddy needed to fix this.

He scrolled down to the last texts, then quickly typed, *I've changed my mind. You shouldn't have to do this, and I don't want you to. I don't want to lie to everyone. So thank you, but you should stay home tonight. I'll tell everyone we broke up, and that way, you don't have to do this. But thank you for being willing to do it. It meant a lot to me.*

Teddy took a deep breath and sent the text, then dropped his phone onto the bed.

He sighed and flopped onto his back, staring at the ceiling. There, he'd done it. He was alone tonight, too, and he would have to face Nysys' disappointment. That didn't matter, though. Even though Nysys was family, he was also a pushy asshole when he wanted to be, which was most of the time. Teddy hated that he felt the need to lie to him and to everyone else, but it wasn't his fault, not entirely. A large part of that fault lay at Nysys' feet, and maybe it was time someone said something to him about that. Teddy probably should have when Nysys had been so pushy about him having a date, but he couldn't. He didn't have the courage to do it, or at least, he hadn't had it until now. It was time to grow up, though. He was about to finish his Master's degree, and since his long-time plans were to eventually open his own accounting firm, he needed to find a job to get experience and learn. He was an adult. He should behave like one.

Another knock on the door made him groan. "What?" he snapped.

"Five minutes have passed," Nysys yelled from behind the door. "I'm coming in."

Teddy hauled himself off the bed. "Don't shimmer in, please. I'm opening the door."

When he did so, he found Nysys waiting for him with his arms crossed over his chest. He looked happy, and Teddy hated to disappoint him, even though he knew this was what would happen from the beginning. "What?" he asked, doing his best to keep his voice steady.

Nysys grinned. "You look cute. Your date is going to be happy."

Teddy shuffled and rubbed the back of his neck. "About that. Ollie texted. He had something else to do, so he won't be able to come. I'm sorry. I know you were looking forward to meeting him, but things are probably better this way. I mean, it's not like we're together. We've just been texting, but it probably wouldn't have come to anything." Teddy couldn't find it in him to tell Nysys they'd broken up, not yet.

Nysys blinked. "What are you talking about?"

"I just told you. Ollie can't come."

"But I just opened the gate for him."

Now it was Teddy's turn to blink. "Excuse me?"

"When I went back downstairs someone rang from the gate. He said he was Ollie, so I opened it for him." Nysys' smile widened. "Maybe he wanted to surprise you. You said he told you he had something else to do?"

Teddy nodded numbly. What the fuck was he going to do

now? "I thought he wasn't coming." He'd hoped so, even after the days that he and Ollie had been texting. Even though he wanted to meet Ollie.

Nysys patted Teddy's shoulder. "Well, he's here, so you better come downstairs. I can't wait to meet him."

Of course, he couldn't. Teddy couldn't, either, and he wasn't sure what to do with that. This was going to be a disaster, wasn't it?

He and Ollie had put together a story, but he didn't feel like it was enough, not anymore. Teddy was terrified someone would realize they'd never met, and that they would tell Jayden and Nysys. Then all hell would break loose, and Teddy would probably get kicked out of the pride or something.

He took a deep breath. No, that wouldn't happen. Dominic wouldn't do that. Teddy might have lied, but it was a white lie that didn't matter. It was a *personal* lie, and Dominic wouldn't do anything about it. He would understand why Teddy had done it.

That didn't change the fact that this was going to be a disaster, though.

Ollie stopped his bike in the parking area in front of the huge house, turned the engine off, and looked up at what was waiting for him.

He could hear music and voices coming from inside, and it made him smile. He was ridiculously eager to meet Teddy, but even if he hadn't been, he was looking forward to meeting new people. He'd always liked that, and parties were the perfect setting for that to happen.

He parked his bike and got off, then took his phone out of his pocket to check his messages. He frowned when he saw one from Teddy, especially when he read it and realized

Teddy had changed his mind. He didn't want Ollie to come anymore, and Ollie wasn't sure what to do. Should he leave? He was sure Teddy would find a way to explain it if he left, but he didn't want to. He wasn't sure what had happened. He needed to talk to Teddy face to face and find out.

He kind of liked the guy, and he'd started wondering if maybe they could have something. He knew Teddy didn't have time for a relationship, and he knew it was ridiculous to hope that he would be different, especially after what Teddy had said about meeting his mate. But hope was the last thing to die and all that. Teddy was a guy Ollie genuinely liked, and he wanted to see where things went between them — if things could even go beyond what they had right now, which was close to nothing.

Before he could make a decision, a pink-haired guy — Nysys — shimmered right in front of him. Ollie blinked at him, then turned his attention to the man who'd shimmered in with the Nix.

Teddy.

He was as adorable as his pictures had shown. His hair was neater tonight, but his glasses were slowly sliding down his nose, and he kept pushing them up as the Nix came closer to Ollie.

"I'm Nysys and aren't you cute." Nysys slapped his hands together. "You two are so adorable together." He dragged the *so* in a way that made Ollie feel like a puppy.

Ollie pushed his phone back into his jeans pocket. "Thanks, I guess? I'm Ollie."

Nysys beamed. "I know that. I couldn't wait to meet you, and now you're here." He turned to Teddy. "Look, he's here."

"I can see that," Teddy mumbled.

He was too adorable for his own good, and Ollie's heart went pitter-patter in a way that couldn't be natural.

"I'm going to leave the two of you alone," Nysys said. He gestured at the house. "Feel free to come in whenever you're ready, of course. The party's already started, and there's food and drinks. I'm sure you need some time alone, though, so I'm going."

Ollie blinked at him. He wasn't sure what he'd expected from what Teddy had told him about this guy, but it wasn't this. Nysys seemed to be generally interested in having Teddy happy, which was probably why he pushed him none too gently toward Ollie and winked before shimmering out.

Ollie had to grab Teddy so he wouldn't fall on his face on the gravel, and he held him close for a second.

It was enough.

Teddy jerked away, his eyes as wide as Ollie's no doubt were. They stared at each other, and Ollie couldn't get Teddy's scent out of his nose. It felt like it was seared there forever, like Ollie would never forget this moment.

But then, how could he forget the moment he'd met his mate?

He supposed he and Teddy hadn't actually met until now. They'd been texting back and forth for several days, which was one of the reasons Ollie was so eager to be here. He wanted to meet the man he'd been talking to. He couldn't wait, actually, and now he understood why he and Teddy seemed to mesh so perfectly together. There was a reason for that, and it wasn't only their personalities.

"We're mates," Ollie said. He wasn't sure why he said it, because Teddy had realized the same thing from how pale he was, but he needed to say the words out loud. Maybe he needed them to feel more real.

Teddy blinked. "You noticed that," he said.

Ollie rolled his eyes. "How am I supposed to *not* to notice it? You were right here in my arms. Of course I did."

Teddy rubbed his face. Then he dropped his hands, and there was a stubborn glint in his gaze. "I'm really sorry about what just happened."

"What are you sorry for?" Ollie asked. He needed to know. He hoped it wasn't that they were mates, but who knew? Teddy had been clear. He'd told Ollie that even if he met his mate, he wouldn't have time for him, and Ollie couldn't imagine how this was going to work.

Was Teddy going to ask him to go home and forget about this moment? Was he going to ask Ollie to wait, maybe until after he found a job? Was he going to want Ollie to stay away entirely?

Ollie hadn't thought about meeting his mate until recently, but now that he had, he wasn't sure what to do. He wanted to push, to make sure Teddy gave him a chance, but could he do that? He didn't want to force his mate into anything Teddy wouldn't want. As of now, it was obvious that what Teddy didn't want was a relationship, and Ollie was having a hard time wrapping his mind around that. Being mates wasn't just any kind of relationship. It was everything, and he didn't want to lose his chance at that.

He should probably ask Teddy about it before starting to freak out, though. Teddy might have said he didn't have time for a mate, but things could be different now that he'd actually met Ollie.

"I'm so sorry for what Nysys did," Teddy said. "He's a good guy, even though he can be pushy and annoying. But you don't have to stay if you don't want to. I'm sure you saw the text I sent you once you arrived here, and I don't have anything else to say about it. I think this is a bad idea, and that you shouldn't have come in the first place. Of course, this isn't your fault. It's entirely mine, and I'll understand if you hate me after this. But I don't think I can continue to lie to my brother, or even to Nysys. They want me to be happy, and for whatever reason, Nysys thinks it's going to happen if I have a boyfriend. He doesn't understand that I'm happy by myself with my books, and that's because we're so different, you know? But anyway, you don't have to stay. I understand that you probably don't want to stick around, especially not now that we found out we're mates." He paused and frowned. "Or maybe you want to stay? We should probably talk about that, to be honest. I didn't expect to meet my mate tonight, and I'm not quite sure what to do. I mean, do you know what to do? Did you even want to meet your mate? Although us meeting doesn't mean we have to be together. You know what I think about meeting my mate right now. Not that I'm rejecting you, because you're a nice guy, and I like you, but I have to focus on school. I'm sorry about that."

Ollie raised a hand. Teddy had been adorable even before he'd started babbling, but even more so now. It was evident that he was overwhelmed, and Ollie got that. He was, too. But they needed to stop talking to each other that way. They needed to have a conversation, and that was going to be hard to do if Ollie couldn't get a word in. "Teddy."

Teddy snapped his mouth shut. "Yes?" he asked hesitantly.

"I'm not going anywhere, not tonight. It's obvious that neither of us expected this to happen, but we need to have a conversation about it. I don't want to force you into anything, especially not into a relationship with me, but you can't deny me a conversation, please. I know what you think about meeting your mate. But now it's happened, and I deserve to hear it from you directly."

Ollie wasn't sure what he was about to hear, but he needed this. He needed Teddy to think about the situation they were in before he made any kind of decision. It wasn't something that might eventually happen one day, not anymore. It was happening right now.

Teddy was babbling, and he was horrified. His brother did

that often, but Teddy had worked hard to make sure he didn't. He wanted people to take him seriously. No one cared when Jayden did it because they were so used to it, but Teddy did his best not to, yet here he was, breaking down in front of his mate.

His *mate*.

He hadn't expected this. He hadn't expected Ollie to be his mate, and he didn't know what to do with it. He couldn't help but think about what he'd told Ollie about meeting his mate. He'd said he didn't want to, and that he wouldn't have time for him. He still didn't, but now that Ollie was in front of him and this was reality, he didn't know what to do.

Teddy couldn't just tell Ollie to leave. He didn't want to, even though he knew that would probably be the best thing to do. He hadn't changed his mind when it came to his studies, and he didn't have time for a relationship. He doubted Ollie would go easily, though. He wanted to talk, and he was right—he deserved a conversation. That was, if Teddy managed to keep his mouth shut for more than five seconds.

Teddy sucked in a breath. "Of course we can talk. You deserve this conversation. I never said you didn't, I'm just trying to say that I'm kind of worried, and I hate that I told you I didn't have time for you, even though I didn't know I was talking about you. I'm sorry about that, and I wish I could take the words back."

Ollie put his hands on Teddy's shoulders. He was smiling, and Teddy wasn't sure why. "Breathe, Teddy."

Teddy blinked. He took a deep breath, briefly closed his eyes, and tried to focus. He needed to stop babbling. He and Ollie were both adults, and they should talk like they were.

When he opened his eyes, Ollie was still looking at him. He was still smiling, too, and the sight made Teddy's breath hitch.

He didn't have time for a mate, and he hated it.

Teddy sighed. "I'm sorry. Thank you for helping me calm down."

Ollie dropped his hands, and Teddy wanted them back on him. The touch had grounded him, had somewhat helped him wrap his mind around what was happening. "It's fine. I know you're shocked. I am, too. And whatever you said in our texts doesn't matter."

Teddy rubbed his face. "But it does. I wasn't lying when I said I didn't have time for relationships. I hate that I told you like that, but it doesn't change the fact that this is the reality. I need to focus on school. I can't allow myself to be distracted, not even by you."

Ollie's expression twisted. "Maybe both of us should take a few days to think things over. I won't continue pushing if you really believe that, but I still think you owe me at least a conversation in which we can try to talk things out. I understand that a relationship will distract you from your studies, and I'm ready to wait if that's what it takes, but not forever. We're mates, Teddy, and that means something to me. I can't say I ever thought I'd meet my mate this way, but I did, and I won't let this go without trying. I just hope you'll do the same. We both deserve it."

He was right. He was right, and it terrified Teddy. He didn't know what to do with a mate. He might have told Nysys he'd had boyfriends in high school, and that hadn't been a lie, but nothing compared to meeting your mate.

And Nysys. Gosh, if he ever found out Ollie was Teddy's mate, he'd be over the moon and tell everyone. Never mind the lie Teddy had told him and Jayden. Never mind that he'd told them that he and Ollie were talking but that they weren't boyfriends. They were freaking *mates*.

"Look, we're supposed to be boyfriends for the evening, right?" Ollie asked.

Teddy nodded. He needed some time to think things out.

His first instinct was to tell Ollie to leave, but Ollie deserved more. Teddy wasn't the only one in this situation, and he couldn't act like he was.

"So let's do this," Ollie continued. "Nothing is going to change over one evening. We're going to go in there, and we're going to act like boyfriends, just like we were supposed to. Once the party is over, I'll go home, and you'll go to your room, or wherever you live. We can take the rest of the night and maybe tomorrow to think, put our thoughts in order. Then maybe we can meet. Or if you want a few more days to think, that's fine too. I pray you'll give us a chance and that you won't close yourself off just because you think you don't have time for me."

Teddy frowned. "But I really don't. I told you, I need to focus—"

"On school. I know. And I'm not asking you to stop doing that. I understand your degree is important to you, even though I never went. But school isn't life. School won't keep you warm at night, and it won't be there for you when you need someone. It won't be there to support you through hard times. I know you have your brother, and no doubt most of the Whitedell pride, and that's fine. But I can offer you much more, and I want us to try. Even if you want to wait until you've graduated, that's okay. I hope you won't close me off from your life. We can start with being friends if that's what you want. The bond is going to push us together, as I'm sure you're aware, but we can ignore it for a bit."

Teddy nodded. He should say something, but he was nowhere near ready to make decisions. Ollie was right—they both needed time to think about this. He was also right when he said that Teddy shouldn't push him away before he took the time to digest the situation and what it meant. He was right that Teddy's first instinct was to close himself off, and that had both to do with his focus on school and with the way his life had gone until now.

The only meaningful relationship in his life was the one he had with his brother. He hadn't had a family since he was thirteen, even though he considered the pride a family. But it wasn't the same. He was terrified to start caring for people and losing them like he'd lost his mother. He wasn't sure how to deal with that, which was why he hadn't until now. But he had to, now that Ollie was in his life.

"Better?" Ollie asked.

The answer was no, but Teddy forced himself to nod. "Thank you," he repeated for what had to be the hundredth time.

Ollie smiled again, and Teddy wished he'd never stop. He was gorgeous, taller than Teddy, with dark hair and a leather jacket that made him look like a forbidden dream.

And he was Teddy's. Teddy might be doing his best to put some distance between them already, but Ollie *was* his mate. There was no denying that.

"We should probably go inside," he murmured. He didn't want to, but staying out here alone with Ollie felt dangerous, as if Teddy might give in. He wanted nothing more than to kiss Ollie right now, to feel Ollie's lips on his own and know that he could have it for the rest of his life.

But he couldn't. He couldn't do that when he still didn't know what he wanted from their relationship. He couldn't allow himself to hurt Ollie. It would be so easy to do that, and Ollie was one of the two people Teddy never wanted to hurt.

Ollie held a hand up. Teddy blinked at it for a second, trying to understand what he meant. Then he did. His hand trembled as he put it into Ollie's, but Ollie's fingers wrapped around his, squeezing. Ollie's presence was strong, and he was telling Teddy that he was there for him, whatever happened.

Teddy was probably fooling himself on that, but he didn't

care. This was what he needed now—Ollie's solid presence, and for everything to be okay, at least for one evening.

If Teddy managed to forget about all his problems for a few hours, he'd be happy.

Ollie had no idea what to think about Teddy or his convictions. He wanted Teddy to give him a chance, and he wanted to give Teddy a chance. He obviously didn't expect them to bond tonight and live together happily ever after, but he would be grateful for at least a step toward that.

He couldn't deny he was mildly offended that Teddy was rejecting him even though they didn't know each other. Being mates didn't mean that people had to rush into mating, especially nowadays. Shifters were out to humans, and even though some of them were still in danger, people had gotten used to them. They didn't have to live closed up in their territories anymore, and now that they were freer, they behaved more like humans. Even when they met their mates, they dated and got to know each other before taking that step. It was very much like a human marriage, except it lasted forever.

Ollie would be more than happy to give Teddy months, or even years to come to terms with what was between them. He didn't want to push him into a relationship he wasn't sure he wanted right now, and both of them were very young. They didn't have to bond right away. They still had more than a hundred years in front of them, and that was more than enough to get to know each other.

So yes, he was slightly angry at the fact that Teddy was saying no right away, or at least that was what it sounded like. He kept repeating that he had to focus on school and that he didn't have time for a relationship, and Ollie didn't believe that. Surely Teddy didn't spend his entire days studying?

Even if he spent hours poring over books, he probably had a private life, friends, a family. Would it be so bad to make space for Ollie in his life?

Still, he'd told Teddy he would play his date tonight, and that was what he'd do, even though he wanted to go home. He didn't deal with rejection well, and Teddy's words felt like one, even though he'd been nice about it.

Nice, and all kinds of adorable.

Ollie hadn't known Teddy tended to ramble when he was nervous. How could he have? He and Teddy didn't know each other. They were meeting for the first time today, and finding out they were mates made everything more complicated. If they hadn't been, Ollie would probably never see Teddy again. He might have wanted to, but he wouldn't have pushed as much as he would now. Once Teddy told him he wasn't ready for a relationship and that he didn't have time for one, he would have taken a step back.

Ollie knew when he wasn't wanted, and he could tell that was the case here. But being mates meant a lot. He wouldn't let Teddy push him away without a good reason, without being sure they couldn't make things work. As of now, the only reason Teddy had not to want Ollie in his life was that he didn't have the time or the focus. He wanted school to be his entire life, and that was okay. School wouldn't last forever.

But Teddy had to realize that and to agree to it. Ollie might not like the idea, but he wouldn't mind taking a step back and giving Teddy space.

So no, Ollie wasn't going anywhere tonight. It wasn't just that he'd promised Teddy he'd play his boyfriend, either. Maybe spending time together tonight would show Teddy that he should give them a chance. Ollie was the first to admit he didn't know what he wanted, but he did know that he should have the chance to find out. Teddy should, too.

Neither of them had arrived this evening thinking they

would meet their mate. Ollie had thought it would be a nice evening at a party, and nothing more. Instead, this evening was life-changing, and he didn't know how yet. Teddy didn't either, but hopefully, he would give both of them a chance to find out.

"Why don't we go inside?" Ollie suggested.

Teddy raked a hand through his hair, or rather, he tried to. But whatever he'd used to do his hair tonight seemed to be hard, and he grimaced when his fingers wouldn't slide through. He took them out and glared at them, and Ollie wished he didn't find everything Teddy did as adorable as he did. "Is that really the best thing we can do? I mean, we haven't talked yet, and you said that was why you're here."

Ollie shook his head. "That's not why I'm here. Yes, I would like to have a conversation with you. I would like to try to convince you to give us a chance, if not now, next week, or next month. I want you to think about it, though. I hope you won't close me out of your life entirely because I don't think I deserve that. Being your mate shouldn't disqualify me from being your friend."

"I never said you couldn't be my friend."

"But you did say you didn't want a mate and that you didn't have time for one."

Teddy huffed. "Relationships are complicated, especially when they first start. People have to find a way around each other, find how they fit together. It takes a lot of time and effort, and no, I don't have the time and focus right now."

Ollie stared at Teddy, trying to understand him. "But surely you have other things in your life that aren't your degree. What about your family?"

"I have a brother."

"And you see him. You love him. I'm sure you talk to him as often as you can."

"Of course I do. He's my brother."

"I'm your mate. Look, I'm not asking to bond with you tonight. That's not realistic, and besides, I wouldn't want that to happen. I need to wrap my mind around all of this too, you know? But I do plan to try to convince you to give me a chance. I don't expect you to say yes, but I hope we can continue texting in the beginning at least. I would also like to take you on a date."

Teddy looked taken aback by that. "You want to date?"

Ollie couldn't help but chuckle at the surprise in his voice. "Yes. Why? What did you think would happen?" Maybe that was why Teddy was terrified. Maybe he had bad experiences with past boyfriends. Ollie really didn't know much about him, and that was the first thing that needed to change between them.

Teddy shrugged. "Honestly? I don't know. It's not like I expected you to be my mate. I thought I'd never see you again after tonight, and I'm not sure I can wrap my mind around all of this."

"And that's exactly why we should continue to text. And I would like to date because you're cute, and I like you from the texts we exchanged. But right now, I'm only here to be a fake boyfriend. That's more than enough. We can talk and get to know each other and eventually reevaluate our relationship. That's all I want. A chance." And he hoped Teddy would give that to him. He wasn't sure what he would do otherwise.

That wasn't true. Ollie knew what would happen—what he would do—if Teddy never wanted to see him again. He'd go home and mope and pout for days, possibly weeks. He might tell Gabriel and his foster parents what had happened, but he wasn't sure. He knew Gabriel would no doubt try talking to Teddy if that was what happened, and Ollie didn't want him to. He didn't want anyone to annoy Teddy or to push him, not if Teddy had already made his decision.

Ollie cleared his throat. "So? What do you think? Are you going to give me a chance?"

Teddy squinted. "And you really don't expect anything else from me? You don't think we should be together, maybe move in together?"

Ollie barked out a laugh. "God, no. We just met ten minutes ago. Why would we move in together already?"

Teddy shrugged. "Maybe because it's what people do when they meet their mates."

"Some people, sure. I don't doubt that some want to bond right away, and that's great if they both agree. But it's obvious you don't, and honestly, me neither. I'm not ready for that kind of relationship. I barely know you. That doesn't change the fact that I want to get to know you. But I don't want more right now. I don't think I could deal with more." Especially not tonight.

Teddy's shoulders slumped, and he looked at the house. "Will you help me tonight, no matter what my answer is?"

Ollie's stomach turned to lead, but he nodded. "Of course."

"Then yes. I'll give you a chance. I can't promise I'll be good at this, that I won't push you away or ignore you, but I'll try."

That was all Ollie had wanted to hear, and all he could take right now.

He squeezed Teddy's hand again. "Shall we go in? I'm sure everyone is waiting to meet your boyfriend."

Teddy groaned. "God, sometimes, I hate Nysys."

CHAPTER FOUR

Jayden's arms wrapped around Teddy. "I'm so happy for you," Jayden murmured.

Teddy forced himself to smile, but he was grateful his brother couldn't see him. "Thank you."

He knew why Jayden was happy, and he hated it. Jayden thought Teddy and Ollie were together, but they weren't. It didn't matter that Ollie was Teddy's mate. Teddy still didn't know what to do with that, and while he had agreed to give Ollie a chance, at least tonight, he couldn't help but feel guilty.

What would happen if Jayden found out he'd lied to him? He would be disappointed, and Teddy didn't think he could bear that.

Jayden leaned away and smiled. "You look nervous. You shouldn't be. He looks like a nice guy, and even if he wasn't, I wouldn't have a say in it. I just wanted you to be happy."

Teddy forced himself to nod. He wasn't sure what it would take to make him happy.

Ollie was Teddy's mate. He could make Teddy happy. But allowing Ollie into his life would mean putting his studies and everything he'd been working so hard for on the back burner, and just the thought made Teddy's stomach churn with nervousness.

Jayden frowned. "What's going on? Did you have a fight outside? Nysys told us your boyfriend had arrived a while ago, but we didn't see you come in, and we all thought you were getting busy."

Teddy shook his head. He didn't want his brother to worry.

"Everything is fine. It's just weird, you know? I mean, Ollie and I met only recently, even though we've been texting. I didn't expect to introduce you to him anytime soon, yet here we are, and it's all Nysys' fault."

Jayden's smile turned indulgent. "That's just Nysys. You know how he is."

Teddy did, and sometimes, he wished someone would say something. He loved Nysys, just like he loved the other pride members. That didn't change the fact that Nysys had invaded his privacy and pushed him into doing something he hadn't planned to do and that he wasn't happy he'd done.

Jayden patted Teddy's back. "You should try to relax for one night. I know you're probably worried about school and that you could get a few hours more of studying in instead of being here, but everyone deserves some time off. You're going to burn out if you don't allow yourself to have fun instead of always having your nose in a book." Jayden chuckled. "And trust me, I understand why you'd want that. I'm more comfortable with books than with most people, and I know the same goes for you. But I don't want you to get hurt, and you're so stressed, especially lately. Take a few hours off, all right?"

Teddy nodded. If anyone else had suggested that, he would have told them he couldn't take the time off, but Jayden was different. He was Teddy's brother, and he was the reason Teddy was doing all this. He was the reason Teddy was focusing so hard on his work, and he wanted to spend time with his brother.

First, though, he needed to find Sterling and Adam. He wasn't sure why he wanted to talk to them since it wasn't like they were friends, but they were the only ones except for Ollie who knew what was going on. Teddy could tell them that Ollie was his mate, and they might help him wrap his mind around it. Or at least, that was what he hoped. He would have talked to his brother usually, but this wasn't something he could tell Jayden.

He finally managed to extricate himself from his brother's arms and looked around. The doors between the living room and the dining room had been opened, and they were both full of people. It made it hard to find someone in particular, and it took Teddy a full minute to recognize Sterling leaning against the wall, laughing and talking to Adam and Adam's brother, Aaron. Teddy made a beeline for them, not bothering to look whether Ollie was following him. Maybe spending some time away from Ollie would be good for him. It wasn't like Ollie was going anywhere tonight anyway.

Teddy didn't want him to go.

Sterling's eyes widened when he saw Teddy coming toward him, and Teddy had to wonder what his expression looked like. "Teddy! You made it." Sterling made a show of looking around. "Where's your boyfriend?"

Teddy shook his head and grabbed Sterling's arm. He dragged him to the side, ignoring the shocked gazes it earned him from Adam and Aaron. "I need to talk to you," he hissed.

Sterling blinked. "What? Isn't Ollie here? He told us he would be."

Teddy shook his head. "He's here, all right." He leaned even closer. He wouldn't get any kind of privacy tonight unless he dragged Sterling to his bedroom, and he wasn't about to do that. "He's my mate."

Sterling jerked away in shock. "He is?"

"Yes. I don't know what to do."

Sterling's smile widened, and he clapped Teddy's back. "That's great!"

Was it, though? Teddy was all over the place when it came to feelings right now.

He should be happy. Most shifters would be in his situation. Meeting Ollie now when he wasn't older than twenty meant he would never have to be alone. Even if for whatever reason he lost his brother — and he knew he wouldn't — Teddy would always have Ollie. They might not know each other well, but he already knew the kind of man Ollie was. He was a good person, as his presence tonight showed. He wouldn't abandon Teddy as long as Teddy made sure not to mistreat him.

And Teddy would have to work on that. He understood his own personality and his limitations well. He knew that he tended to close himself off from everyone but Jayden when he was worried. It had to do with his past, just like everything else in his life. But he'd always been alone. He'd always only had his brother and his mother until Jayden left and she died.

It was easier to be alone. It was easier not to trust anyone because they could hurt you if you did.

And Ollie would hurt Teddy. Apart from Jayden, he was the only one who had that ability. Teddy didn't know how to accept that or what to do with the knowledge. No matter how much he trusted Ollie — and it wasn't much right now since they didn't know each other — he knew that Ollie would hurt him, and he would hurt Ollie. He needed to decide if what a relationship with Ollie would offer was enough to go through that or not.

It was hard to force himself to trust, and Teddy wasn't sure he could do it. He found that he wanted to, though, and he was surprised with himself. Maybe being on his own, focusing on nothing but his degree, had been a mistake. It had been the easy way out for him, but possibly not the right one.

"Teddy?" Sterling asked. He wasn't smiling anymore.

"I'm fine. Just all over the place, you know?"

The smile was back on Sterling's face. "Yeah, I remember how it was to meet Adam. Of course, it wasn't the same."

"How did you do it? You're even younger than me. Didn't you think that meeting Adam so young would ruin all your plans for the future?"

Sterling blinked. "Ruin them? No, of course not. I knew it wouldn't be easy to include him in my life, and I obviously didn't expect to have to take care of my siblings and lose my parents, but I'm so freaking glad I had him when it happened. I don't know what I would have done if I'd been alone." He hesitated. "You know, some people think that's why we meet our mates."

Teddy had heard the legend, story, or whatever he wanted to call it. "They think you meet your mate when you most need him or her."

"Exactly. And I think it makes sense. I mean, they're the person who more than anyone will be there for you, support you, things like that. I know I would have had the support of the pack even if I didn't have Adam, but it wouldn't have been the same. Honestly, I'm glad I met him, even though we're so young." His smile widened. "And I'm glad you met Ollie. I can't say I expected this to happen, but it's good, right?"

Teddy was starting to wonder.

Everyone he knew, everyone he could talk to, was happy in their relationship with their mates. For some of them, it had taken some time and a lot of work, but that didn't change the result. Could Teddy and Ollie have that? Could Teddy put his studies on the back burner and focus on Ollie?

Because that was what Ollie deserved. Teddy had repeated again and again to him that he needed to focus on his studies, that he couldn't allow himself to be distracted, and that was true. But he also didn't want to give Ollie too little attention. Ollie was his mate, and he deserved to be Teddy's focus, especially now that they'd just met.

Teddy didn't know if he could do that. He didn't know if he wanted to try. He didn't know if he could allow himself to trust Ollie. Ollie could hurt him. He could crush Teddy's heart to pieces, and Teddy would never be able to put it back together.

But Teddy needed to make a decision, even though Ollie had told him to wait. He couldn't live wondering if what he was doing was the right or the wrong thing to do.

Ollie knew exactly where Teddy was. It was as if his gaze was attracted to his mate, and he hadn't expected that. It was a good thing, though. He needed to keep an eye on Teddy, if anything because he knew Teddy was panicking.

Teddy was doing his best to hide it, and he was doing a good job. Ollie didn't think Teddy's brother had noticed he wasn't as happy as he showed, but that made sense, considering everyone was distracted tonight. The party was great—great music, good food, and a lot of people. Ollie felt like he'd talked to about a hundred of them, even though he knew that couldn't be right. There was no way a hundred people could fit into these rooms, even though they were packed.

But even with so many people there, he kept an eye on Teddy. He didn't miss the way Teddy panicked after talking to his brother, and how he made a beeline for Sterling and Adam. Ollie hadn't realized those three were friends, although it made sense. Sterling had been the one who'd suggested Ollie do this, after all.

"Everything all right?" Nysys asked, suddenly appearing in front of Ollie.

Ollie jumped a little, and it made Nysys laugh. Ollie scowled at him, even though he wasn't angry. "I'm great. Just a bit overwhelmed. I don't know a lot of people here."

Nysys nodded as if he knew how Ollie felt. "It's the first time you've been here, right?"

"It is. I don't have friends in Whitedell."

"How did you meet Teddy, then?"

"Sterling and Adam. I'm not exactly friends with them, but I know them. We're part of the same pack. He's friends with them, and they introduced us."

Nysys' expression twisted and became sappy. "That's so cute. You two are adorable together."

Ollie rubbed the back of his neck. "Thanks, I guess."

"I guess?"

"I'm almost thirty. I don't want to be adorable. But I can't deny Teddy is."

Nysys laughed. "God, he is. I have to say I'm surprised you managed to take him away from his books for so long. I mean, it's been what? Almost an hour by now?"

Ollie frowned. "His studies are important to him."

Nysys waved Ollie's words away. "Of course they are, and it's a good thing. But what is *not* a good thing is if he allows himself to burn out. That boy has been in school for years already. I know because while I don't live here, I do spend most of my time in the house with the pride. He's been laser-focused the entire time, and I doubt he's given himself more than one day off since he started, not even when he was sick. And that day off I'm talking about? That only happened because he looked like he was about to die and Jayden forced him to take care of himself."

Ollie frowned. He knew how focused Teddy was, of course, but he couldn't help but worry. "You think he's going to burn out?"

Nysys shrugged. "It's bound to happen eventually. I mean, everyone tries to take him away from his books for at least a few hours every day, but no one succeeds except his brother. It took a minor miracle for him to agree to come to this party. I'm pretty sure he only came because of you."

"You told him you'd find him a date if he didn't have one."

Nysys wrinkled his nose. "I did. I know I was pushing. I won't deny that. But it's because I'm worried about him. I honestly thought that having a boyfriend might help him relax and get distracted for a bit. He deserves that, and more importantly, he *needs* it."

Ollie hadn't been sure what to think of Nysys when Teddy had talked about him, but now, he was sure Nysys cared about Teddy, and no doubt, about all the pride members. He might not have gone about it the right way, but he really worried.

"It's good that he has you," Nysys continued. "I don't expect you to work miracles. I don't think anyone can. But forcing him to take a few hours off in the evening, and possibly an entire weekend, can only do him good. I hate to think that once he finishes his degree, his entire focus will shift to his work. He's exactly the kind of person who would do something like that, and that's going to be even worse than with school."

"Thanks for the heads up."

Nysys shrugged. "I don't think you needed it. I have to say, I was surprised when Teddy said he was bringing you, but I'm glad he did. You look like a nice guy."

Ollie wasn't sure how to answer. He thought he was a decent guy, even though he was here on a lie. Or was it?

He and Teddy had been telling people they were *talking*. Not that they were dating, or that they were boyfriends. And they *had* been talking. They'd been texting ever since Sterling had given Ollie Teddy's number.

And now, they'd found out they were mates.

This was the exact situation they'd told everyone they were in, and they were, now.

Everything had changed the moment Ollie had seen Teddy for the first time.

He looked around again, but Teddy wasn't with Sterling and Adam anymore. Ollie frowned, then jerked when someone tapped him on the shoulder.

"Go get him," Nysys said. "And warn him that if I see him with a book in his hands, I'm taking all of them away. And I'm not kidding. That boy needs the entire weekend to relax, and I'm going to make sure that's what he does."

Ollie nodded without answering. He didn't know if Nysys would keep that promise, and he didn't want to find out. He *did* want to find Teddy, though, so he made his way toward Sterling and Adam, who were talking in the corner with a younger man. The guy had to be eighteen or nineteen, if even that, and he had a pair of impressive wings on his back. Ollie blinked at them, but he didn't dare ask. Besides, he was more interested in finding Teddy.

Sterling smiled at him when he saw him approach. "Teddy told me," he said. "Congratulations?"

Ollie chuckled. "I'm not quite sure about that yet, but thank you. Teddy and I are still trying to figure things out."

Sterling nodded. "That's what he told me. He's a little frantic, right?"

"Well, it was a surprise. Neither of us expected this to happen."

"Isn't that how it always goes, though? I didn't expect to meet Adam, but I'm grateful I did when I did like I told Teddy. I'm sure there's a reason you two met now, and I hope that knowledge will help him accept it."

Ollie looked around. "Do you know where he went?"

"Outside. He said he needed some air."

Ollie grimaced. He didn't like that. He didn't want Teddy to have more time to dwell on his thoughts. He already knew that Teddy didn't want him in his life, not right now, maybe not for weeks or months, and while he was ready to fight against that, he wasn't sure he could. Giving Teddy even more time to think about it and try to find a way around Ollie's presence in his life wasn't a good thing for Ollie. "Thank you. I'll go find him."

Sterling nodded. "Good luck."

Ollie was going to need it.

He made his way toward the back door. It was open and letting in fresh air that smelled of roses. The air outside was cool, but it felt good after the overheated house.

Ollie looked around, but he couldn't see Teddy, not at first. Then he saw a pair of legs sticking out from behind two bushes, and he made his way there. He could only see Teddy's jeans and his shoes, but he knew it was him.

He found Teddy sitting on a stone bench between rose-bushes. The setting made him even more gorgeous, and Ollie gave himself a moment to take everything in.

This man was his mate. If everything went the right way, Ollie would be spending the rest of his life with him. The thought was as terrifying as it was exhilarating.

"Teddy?" he called softly.

Teddy still jerked. "Hey. How did you find me?"

"Sterling told me you were outside. Everything okay?"

Teddy shrugged. Everything wasn't okay, and Ollie understood that.

"Can I sit with you?" Ollie asked.

"Of course."

Ollie did. They both stayed silent for a moment, and Ollie tried to find a way to say what he was thinking. "I'm sorry."

He could see Teddy frown in the light coming out of the windows. "What are you sorry about?"

"I know this is messing up your life, and that's the last thing I wanted to do. I also understand that you need me to step away, and that's what I will do if you haven't changed your mind."

Teddy frowned. "I don't get it. What are you saying?"

Ollie had said both of them should take some time to think about this, so he was probably making a mistake—possibly the biggest mistake in his life—but he hated to see Teddy hurting the way he was. "I don't want to push you into some-thing you don't want, and it's obvious you don't want me in your life, not right now. If that's what you want, I'll leave."

Teddy didn't know what he wanted. He never allowed him-self to think about it. He'd always focused on making Jayden proud of him, and that meant a degree, then a good job.

He would have said yes to any other man who'd told him he would leave. He would have told him he didn't have time for this.

But Ollie wasn't just a guy. He was Teddy's mate, and Teddy didn't want to lose that, no matter how focused he was on school, or maybe because of it.

Because Ollie was right. His degree was important, as was finding a job, but it couldn't be the center of Teddy's world. Teddy hadn't entirely realized how much he was isolating himself until now, but he couldn't deny it anymore. The fact that he'd contemplated pushing his mate away and getting rid of him was horrifying.

He would never find someone like this again. Ollie was his one and only mate, and if Teddy lost him, he wouldn't get a second chance. No matter what Ollie said, no matter how much he tried to reassure Teddy that he could give him time, Teddy wasn't sure he believed that.

How could Ollie not become bitter if Teddy rejected him? Even if he tried convincing himself that it was only for a few months or a few years, it was bound to hurt him, and that was the last thing Teddy wanted.

Yes, Teddy needed to focus on his degree and finding a job, on making his brother proud, but maybe Jayden didn't need him to be the first of his class or the best paid guy. Maybe Jayden wanted him to be happy, and that would be enough to make him proud.

Teddy needed to have a talk with his brother, but he couldn't do that now. Ollie was waiting for an answer, and Teddy needed to give him one.

He nodded before he could think about what Ollie might get from that. He didn't realize that Ollie would take it as a yes, as Teddy's answer that he should leave, until Ollie was rising from the bench. His expression was shattered as if Teddy had hurt him, and Teddy realized he *had*. He'd just told his mate he didn't want him, even though that wasn't what he'd been trying to do.

He caught Ollie's wrist before Ollie could leave and pulled him back. Ollie stumbled, then turned around, his eyes wide.

Teddy swallowed. "Sit down. I don't want you to leave. Please."

Ollie didn't look convinced, but he obeyed. He settled back onto the bench next to Teddy and waited. Teddy didn't doubt that Ollie wanted an explanation, and he had to give him one.

Ollie deserved it.

Teddy swallowed. "I've always thought that the only way to make my brother proud of me was to succeed in life, and for me, succeeding in life is finding a good job, earning a lot of money, so that I will never have to depend on anyone else. When I was a kid, our alpha wasn't a good man. He used his power over us to keep us in line, and Jayden had to leave because he was gay. I knew I was, too, but I was terrified of losing everything. I was only a kid. Then my mother died. I was lucky enough that she gave me Jayden's phone number, but I don't know what I would have done if I hadn't been able to contact him. I would probably have ended up on the streets or beaten into submission by someone stronger than me. I don't know, and I don't want to think about it. It's in the past. But I can't deny that the past influences the way I act now, the way I think. I'll always be afraid to be alone. I'll always be afraid to trust people and to let them have power over me. I'm terrified of allowing you into my life because you could hurt me. Other than Jayden, you're probably the one person who could do that, who could kill me with a gesture. So that's one of my problems. I'm also terrified of what you might ask from me if I agree to be with you. I know you're not the kind of man who's going to ask me to stay home with our kids, or at least I don't think so, but my heart doesn't understand that. It's stuck on the fact that as my mate, you have power over me."

To Teddy's surprise, Ollie reached over and took his hand. He gently squeezed, and Teddy's heart broke a bit.

He'd never wanted to hurt Ollie. It had been so easy to shield himself as soon as he realized Ollie was his mate. It had been easy to hide inside his shell, tried to ignore the bond they shared. Neither of them had had time to think about it, but Teddy couldn't deny the way he behaved. He'd pushed Ollie away before even giving him a chance, and he was about to lose his mate because of that. He was a mess, but a mess Ollie seemed to want, and Teddy didn't know why.

"I understand everything you've explained," Ollie said. "I hate that you had to go through that. I also realize that none of my promises is going to be enough for you to trust me. And you're not wrong. Sometimes, the people we trust hurt us. It's life, and you're going to have to accept dealing with that if you want any kind of significant relationship. So far, you've limited yourself to your brother. You trust him, even though you know he could hurt you."

Teddy shook his head. "Jayden would never hurt me."

"He wouldn't do it on purpose, sure. But he might say or do something you're not okay with. But that's the point with people you trust and love. If they do something to hurt you, you go to them and you tell them. You explain why it hurts, and together, you find a way to patch things up. That's what I want."

Teddy slowly nodded. "I get that. I really do. But I need you to understand how hard it is for me to shift gears. I've been focused on making my brother proud. But I talked to him earlier, after you arrived, and he's happy for me. He's proud of me for finally finding love, and I felt like shit when I realized that he thought we were together. I mean, I was the one who told him that, so of course, he believed it, and at this point, it's not a lie anymore, but you get what I mean. He's happy for me because he thinks I'm dating you, and he wants that to continue. He told me to focus on you for a while. He didn't exactly say I should forget my degree, and he knows I wouldn't even if he suggested it, but he did mention that maybe I could have another focus in life. And you were right. A degree and a good job aren't going to make me happy, not in the long run. They aren't going to be part of my life forever, and I won't be able to build a family with them. They're not a person, but you are. I should have seen that earlier."

Ollie shook his head. "I think you're too hard on yourself."

Teddy blinked. "You do? I mean, you thought I was pushing you away just now. You were going to leave without pushing. And I know that's my fault. It's because of what I told you and the way I behaved. But it hurts."

"I wasn't going to leave forever."

"You started to leave!"

Ollie rubbed his face without letting go of Teddy's hand. "You're right, I did. But what I meant was that I would go for the next few days, or weeks before trying to contact you again. If you were rejecting me, I wanted to give you time to think about this and realize what you might lose. I think I already told you this, but I'm ready to wait for as long as you need for you to be ready. If you want to finish your degree before we start dating, then that's fine. If you want to find a job before we do, that's fine, too. Both of us are young, and we have a lot of time in front of us. I wouldn't mind giving you some. I don't want to force you into anything or to freak you out."

Teddy wasn't sure how he'd gotten so lucky. Ollie was understanding, much more so than he should be. Many other people would have told Teddy to stop freaking out and make a decision already, but Ollie wasn't. He was giving Teddy time and space, and Teddy wasn't sure he needed them anymore, even though they'd just met.

Ollie was a good man. Teddy hadn't allowed himself to see that before, or rather, he'd conveniently blocked it out as soon as he'd realized Ollie was his mate. But he and Ollie had started getting to know each other over texts ever since Sterling had given Ollie Teddy's number. Ollie was smart. He was funny, and he was a good person. Teddy could see how Ollie would fit perfectly in his life.

He would help him focus on things that weren't books and exams. He would give him a much-needed lightness, something to think about when he needed a break.

Teddy didn't have to get rid of Ollie to be able to find a job. Hundreds, *thousands* of people did that every day.

But Teddy needed to stop freaking out at the thought of letting Ollie into his life. He'd conveniently hidden behind the school and job excuses, but they were just that.

Excuses.

Ollie wanted to continue talking and to convince Teddy to open up to him, but this was something Teddy had to do alone. At least he was starting to realize that his entire focus couldn't be his work for the rest of his life. Ollie supposed it was a step forward, but he wasn't sure how much it would help.

Teddy tried to rake a hand through his hair and scowled when he couldn't. "I shouldn't have used this much gel."

"You don't usually?" Ollie asked. Maybe they should

continue talking about their relationship and what would happen, or maybe he could give Teddy a few minutes to gather his thoughts and talk about something that didn't matter.

Teddy shook his head. "I don't usually do anything with my hair. I tend to pull on it and rake my hand through it when I study, which is what I do most days. It wouldn't make sense to style it." Teddy sucked in a breath. "And I'm sorry about my babbling. It's a family thing. My brother does it too when he's nervous, and even though I've been trying my hardest not to do it, with you, it just comes out."

Ollie thought it was kind of adorable. Sure, it made it hard to have a conversation with Teddy since he couldn't get a word in, but it was sweet. He didn't like that Teddy was nervous with him, but he understood why. Besides, he was pretty quiet himself. He didn't mind listening to Teddy talking for both of them, especially when he shared Teddy's opinions.

"Teddy," Ollie began. He wasn't sure how to continue, though. "I don't want you to make decisions you might regret. That means that I don't expect you to decide anything right now. We only met a few hours ago, even though we've texted a lot. But I do want to date you. I'm ready to wait for you if that's what you want. I just want to be sure that I won't lose you if we wait. It seems to me that it's easy for you to focus on work and your degree because those two things can't disappoint you. But I'm not one of them. I'm a person, and I'm sure that if we do end up together, I'll hurt and disappoint you many times. I'll do my best not to do it, but I'm only human."

"I know that."

Ollie nodded. "I guess that what I'm trying to say is that I don't want you to push me away only because you're afraid. You've been keeping everyone but your brother away because you're so afraid of being out of control and hurt, but you can't live your entire life like that. I don't want to wait for years if I don't have a certainty that you're at least trying to deal with it. I'm your mate, but I won't wait forever." Even though Ollie wanted to say he would.

Because what were the odds that he would eventually forget Teddy? *Zero.* Teddy was Ollie's mate, and even if he rejected Ollie, that would never change. Even if they never saw each other again, if they never bonded, if they never spoke to each other, the bond wouldn't disappear. It would always be between them. Now that Ollie knew it was there, he wouldn't be able to forget that, and he wasn't sure he wanted to.

No matter how hard this was, how confusing and overwhelming, he wanted Teddy. He wanted to help Teddy realize how unbalanced his life was, to help him deal with it.

Teddy peered at Ollie, and Ollie held his breath. He wasn't sure how long it took Teddy to finally nod, but it was kind of confusing, so Ollie asked, "What does that mean?"

Teddy nodded again. "That you're right. I've been using school to hide because I know that it can't hurt me. I don't depend on it. You're different. Human beings are different. But life comes with pain, doesn't it? I've already been through a lot, and I've lost my mother. The thought of losing you is terrifying, even though we barely know each other."

"And you think that by staying away, things will be easier? You're ready to lose me so that you won't hurt over losing me."

Teddy snorted. "I get what you're asking, even though it doesn't make much sense. But yes. I guess that it's easier to push you away now than trying this and possibly losing you in the future."

Ollie wanted to promise he wasn't going anywhere, but he couldn't. Even though they were mates, it didn't mean they would end up together, or that they would bond. Those cases were rare, but it did happen that some mates broke up or never found a way to share the lives.

Ollie wasn't sure this could work, but he wanted it to. They would both have to work on it, though. Ollie didn't know if Teddy would be able to do that. No matter how much he said he could, he was still hesitant. He was still *afraid*. Ollie understood that, and he hoped he wasn't making the wrong decision by agreeing to this, whatever *this* was.

"I want us to date," Teddy said.

Ollie wondered if Teddy was trying to convince himself of that by repeating it. "You do?"

"I do. You're right, and so is my brother, and as much as I hate to admit it, I shouldn't hide behind my degree anymore. I'm not going to lose you. You're not going to hurt me."

Ollie opened his mouth to tell Teddy that he still might, but Teddy waved his words away.

"You know what I mean. I'm sure that whatever happens between us, you'll talk to me and try to work things out."

Ollie had already lost a lot. He'd never known his father, and his mother was flighty and had never really cared about him. But even with that bad start in life, he'd found a family. He had his foster parents and his foster siblings. He would never be alone, even if Teddy broke up with him.

And the same went for Teddy. He would always have his brother, and from the looks of it, the pride.

"It's not going to be easy," Teddy continued.

Ollie was starting to realize that nothing would ever be with Teddy, except maybe loving him. He could see himself fall in love so easily with his mate. Teddy felt everything so strongly, but he was fragile and vulnerable. Ollie wanted to protect him, even though Teddy was an adult. And he thought that Teddy needed that protection. He'd been trying to be strong on his own for so long that he didn't realize he didn't have to. He could lean on Ollie, let Ollie be his rock, just like Ollie could do with him.

If they wanted this to work, they had to admit that they were both vulnerable and sometimes, they would need each other. That was the point of being a couple.

Ollie brought Teddy's hand to his lips and kissed the back of it. He liked how wide Teddy's eyes went, but he needed to finish this conversation before he did anything else. "Let's start dating. We can begin with an evening per week, maybe. We can continue to text, and I'll pick you up on Saturday so we can go out. We'll get to know each other, and you'll see that I can mesh into your life. I'm not saying I won't be a distraction because I suspect I will be, just like you will be for me. But that's life. You can't always close yourself off when you need to focus on something, and you have to learn that. I'm going to try my best not to interfere with your studies, but I'm not backing out of this, not now that I know you don't want me to."

Teddy nodded. His gaze was still fixed on Ollie's lips, and Ollie yearned to kiss him. He waited until Teddy said what he had to say, though.

"All right. Let's date and see where things go. Neither of us will make any decision before we talk again, okay?"

"Okay. We can do it like that." Ollie prayed he wouldn't hurt Teddy while they dated, that Teddy would see how well they could work together.

He had no idea what the future would be like for them, but he wanted Teddy in his life, and he was ready to do pretty much anything to make that happen. He might not have known about his mate until tonight, but he did now, and Teddy meant a lot to him just because of that. That, and the fact that Ollie liked Teddy from their texts and from the little time they'd spent together, would make it easy for Ollie to stick around as long as Teddy didn't push him away.

He leaned closer, giving Teddy the time to move away if he didn't want to be kissed, but Teddy didn't budge. His eyes were still wide, and he licked his lips when Ollie was almost touching them. Ollie heard him suck in a breath and hold it, and it made him chuckle. He didn't want Teddy to faint because he wasn't breathing, so he quickly brushed their lips together in their first kiss.

"That's it?" Teddy asked as Ollie moved back.

Ollie laughed, feeling so much lighter than he had before. "For now. Do you want me to kiss you some more?"

Ollie didn't want to push, so he needed Teddy to take a step toward him, toward *them.*

Teddy nodded, and to Ollie's surprise, he wrapped an arm around Ollie's neck and pulled him forward. "I hope this will only be the first kiss in a long, infinite, series of them," Teddy murmured before kissing Ollie again.

Ollie hoped the same thing. It was too soon for anything else, but God, he wanted to find out what the future with Teddy would be like. "Why don't we go back inside?" he murmured.

Teddy shook his head. "I don't want to." He bit his lower lip. "What kind of shifter are you?"

Ollie blinked at the unexpected question. "A hedgehog." He was wary to admit it. He knew plenty of people who made fun of him when they found out a big guy like him shifted into a tiny animal.

But Teddy's smile just grew, and it wasn't unkind. "I'm a weasel shifter. We're the perfect size for each other, even in our animal forms. Do you want to go play in the forest? I don't know about you, but I'm not looking forward to going back inside. It's too hot, and there are too many people."

Ollie couldn't think of a more perfect thing to do. He rose from the bench and offered Teddy his hand, his smile widening when Teddy took it. "Lead the way."

Teddy did. They walked to the edge of the forest, and Ollie wasn't surprised to find a chest that could be opened to put clothes in. The pack had something similar for when its members wanted to shift away from their home.

He carefully avoided looking at Teddy as they both stripped and shifted, even though he wanted to see what his mate looked like naked. He'd have time to find out when they got to know each other better, and he couldn't wait.

Ollie rolled his back as soon as he was in his hedgehog form. Something touched his butt, making him jump, and he twirled around and hissed. A weasel jumped back, and Ollie would have laughed at the look on Teddy's face if he could have. He wanted to tell his mate he was sorry for startling him, so he reached out with his nose and gently rubbed it against Teddy's.

It was easier to be with Teddy like this. It gave both of them a moment to relax and stop thinking about what had happened, and that was exactly what they needed, so Ollie bumped his nose against Teddy's again, then turned around and ran away as fast as he could.

He might not have been able to smile physically, but when he heard Teddy coming after him, he did so in his mind.

Chapter Five

Teddy had known this would happen from the first time he'd realized Ollie was his mate. He'd known this was a possibility, yet he'd decided to go along with it and date Ollie.

And now, here he was, trying to study but unable to focus on the books he loved so much.

He sighed and pushed away from the desk. He'd known this would happen, yet he couldn't find it in himself to regret it. He might not have the slightest idea what he was doing with Ollie, and he might not be able to study, but he'd also never been so happy, except maybe when he'd been thirteen and Jayden had rescued him and brought him home. This was a different kind of happiness, one Teddy had never allowed himself to experience, and now, he wasn't sure he could do without it.

Yes, he couldn't stop thinking about Ollie. But it didn't mean it was a bad thing. He might be trying to study, but if he was honest with himself, he could admit that he already knew all this stuff. He'd been studying so much over the past years that it had become easy for him. He was distracted, but it didn't detract from his studies.

"What's going on?" Jayden asked from the bed. Teddy's brother was visiting along with his mate, but Heath was somewhere in the house, no doubt talking about something or other with one of his friends. Jayden, on the other hand, had always been more reserved, even though he babbled a lot. He came to Whitedell often to visit with Teddy, and Teddy enjoyed having him in his bedroom when he studied.

Of course, that meant that Jayden could see how distracted Teddy was, and he knew it wasn't what Teddy was usually like.

Teddy twisted his chair around so he could see his brother. "I'm distracted."

Jayden snorted loudly. "I can see that. I don't think I've ever seen you like this, not even when you were a teenager still trying to finish high school. So again, what's going on?"

Teddy hesitated. He didn't want to lie to Jayden a second time, so going along with the tale that Ollie was just his date or even his boyfriend was out. But Teddy hadn't yet told anyone but Sterling and Adam that Ollie was his mate, even though he should have. He should have told Jayden right away.

But since he didn't want to lie to Jayden again, this wasn't going to be easy.

He licked his lips. "Okay. Don't be angry at me."

Jayden frowned and sat up, crossing his legs and facing Teddy. "You know that if you start a sentence with *don't get angry*, I'm bound to get angry, right? That, and it's making me worry even more. Do you have a problem? Are you in trouble?"

Teddy shook his head. Of course his brother's mind would go straight there. "I'm not in trouble, I promise. It's quite the opposite, actually, at least if you consider my previous life. My studies might be in trouble, but I'll make sure that doesn't happen."

"Why don't you get straight to the point and tell me what's going on? Then we can discuss it. I hate feeling like I don't understand what you're talking about."

"It's Ollie," Teddy started.

Jayden arched a brow. "Your boyfriend?" He raised his hands. "Sorry, your *date*. You two are *not* together, as you made a point of telling me."

Teddy ignored his brother's snark. "That's the thing. We are together. We started dating the night of the party. And that's not all." Teddy took a deep breath and threw himself off the cliff—figuratively, but he did feel like he might lose a lot after the next few words were said. "He's my mate."

Jayden blinked slowly. He was usually very chatty, especially with Teddy because he trusted him and felt comfortable with him, so Teddy was worried when his brother didn't open his mouth right away to ask him questions or maybe berate him for not telling him before.

Teddy swallowed. "He's the reason I can't focus. That, and the fact that we're mates. I'm terrified that not being able to focus on my studies is going to ruin everything. I know that's not the case. I know that will only happen if I let it. But I've never been in a serious relationship, and Ollie isn't just a guy." Teddy raked a hand through his hair. Now that he was talking about it, this felt much bigger than he'd been trying to convince himself of until now. "What am I doing? I'm ruining my chances to make it out of school at the top of the class."

Jayden raised his hands again, seemingly finally getting out of his funk. "Slow down, Teddy. What are you talking about? Why would meeting your mate and dating him ruin your chances at school? That doesn't make sense."

Teddy sighed and tried to get his breathing under control. He knew that. He knew Jayden was right, but it was so easy to allow panic to take over. "I've only ever tried to make you proud of me," Teddy murmured. "That's why I graduated high school with the highest grades possible. That's why I'm doing my best to finish my degree first in my class. And I'm planning to find a good job that pays well. All because of you. Because I want you to be proud of me. I never want you to regret saving me when I was thirteen. You could have decided to put me in a foster home or something like that, but instead, you and your mate welcomed me into your home, and you gave me a second chance. You gave me a real chance at life, and I will never be able to repay you for that."

Jayden jumped off the bed and rushed to Teddy. He threw himself on his knees next to him and grabbed his hands, squeezing so hard it hurt. "What are you talking about? I've always been proud of you, and it has nothing to do with your studies or how high your grades are."

He paused and cocked his head. "Well, it does kind of have to do with that. I won't say I wasn't proud to see how well you did in school, and now in grad school, but that's not the main reason I'm proud of you. I'm proud of you because of who you are. I'm proud of you because of the way you managed to leave the past behind. Neither of us started well in life. Mom loved us, but with the alpha and everything else, we never had a chance. It would have been so easy to lose you, even after I found you, but instead, you pushed through, and you're still here. You're a good person, and that's the most important thing. I've only ever wanted you to be happy, and I never said much about you obsessing over studying because I thought *that* was what made you happy. Especially since you moved out, it's not like I know what kind of relationship you have with people. I don't see them, and I thought you had people in your life. But Nysys has been talking to me, and he mentioned that Ollie was your first relationship ever since you moved in. I've been worried."

Teddy shook his head. "You don't have to be worried. It's true Ollie is my first relationship, but then, how could it be otherwise? It's not like I can push him away. He's my mate."

"But you could. You could isolate yourself even more than you've already been doing. I wouldn't have been surprised if you had. But instead, you're pushing through that, too. You want to be happy, and you're finally realizing that I don't care about your grades. I care about *you*, and about you being happy. I wouldn't even care if you decided to drop out of school."

Teddy sucked in a breath. "Drop out of school?"

Jayden laughed and shook his head. "I'm not saying that you have to do that. But if you decided to do that, I wouldn't care. I don't think that a person's worth depends on where they went to college or how high their grades were. It depends on who they are and how they act, and you're a good person. That's all that matters to me."

Teddy couldn't help but smile. "That, and me being happy."

Jayden beamed. "Exactly. So, does Ollie make you happy?"

Teddy took a moment to think about it. He had to. He'd already lied to his brother once, and he didn't want to do it again. He never wanted to feel that way again. "I guess he does. I'm just not used to all of this, you know? I've been forcing myself to focus only on my degree for so many years that I'm not sure how to act in this relationship. I already knew I'd be more distracted than usual, and sometimes, I can't deny that it feels like it's too much."

"But you're not pushing Ollie away, are you?"

Teddy shook his head. "I want to sometimes. I think it would be the easiest way out of this. But then I remember that me and Ollie talked, and he was so vulnerable, so afraid he'd lose me, and I can't do it to him. I don't want to lose him. I know that's what would happen if I pushed him away, so when I panic, I try to think of something else. I take a walk or something like that." And more often than not, Nysys found him, of course. But Teddy hadn't told him how worried he was, or that Ollie was his mate. Jayden deserved to hear it first, and now he had.

Jayden patted his knee. "Good man. Give him a chance, and if you really have trouble focusing, or any other problem, talk to him. He's your mate. He'll understand, or rather, he *should* understand. If he doesn't, that means you two shouldn't be together."

Teddy had no doubt Ollie would understand if Teddy talked to him. He couldn't put school on Ollie's shoulders, though, not when he had nothing to do with it. It was something that Teddy had to do alone, but it felt good to know that he had support.

Ollie would never push Teddy away for this. He was giving Teddy all the time he needed to study. He wasn't texting him or calling, not in the middle of the day. He always waited until after dinner because he said that that was when Teddy needed a distraction the most. Teddy couldn't deny he was right. He'd been sleeping better now that he didn't obsess over books right until the moment he went to bed.

Ollie was changing Teddy's life, and even though Teddy had been terrified in the beginning, it was for the best, not for the worse.

Ollie had his head inside a bike — or as close as he could come to it anyway — when he heard someone walk in. "Just a second," he yelled without looking at the person.

He finished what he was doing before straightening up. He grabbed the rag he used to clean his hands, thinking that it was time to hire Cyn. He didn't have a reason not to. He'd asked Cyn to work on one of the bikes recently, and he'd checked over his work. The man was good. The only reason Ollie hadn't hired him yet was that he'd been busy thinking about Teddy and everything else. He'd been distracted. But he needed help now.

He turned to welcome the customer, his eyes widening when he saw it was Teddy. "What are you doing here?"

Teddy arched a brow. "You don't sound happy to see me."

"Of course I'm happy to see you. I just didn't expect you to come. Has something happened?"

Teddy huffed. "Why is everyone asking that? No, nothing has happened. I'm okay. I couldn't focus on my books, and I talked with my brother. He pointed out that maybe staying away from you during the week wasn't helping since I couldn't focus anyway, so here I am." He raised the backpack he'd been carrying on his shoulder. "I hope you don't mind if I sit somewhere and study."

Ollie looked around. He didn't have a place for Teddy to sit. There was an old couch in a corner, but the thing was dirty as hell. It was where Ollie rested when he worked between one bike and another, and it wasn't fit for Teddy.

But Teddy didn't seem to care. He noticed the couch and headed there before Ollie could say anything. He flopped onto it after dropping his bag, and he looked strangely happy.

This wasn't what Ollie had expected. He and Teddy had been texting, but only in the evening when Ollie was sure he wouldn't disturb Teddy. They'd seen each other once, and it had gone well, but Ollie wasn't willing to let himself hope yet. Teddy was trying, that much was obvious. But they were both still hesitant, and that was okay. It was normal.

But now, Teddy was here.

Ollie cleared his throat. "Of course. I would have offered already if I'd known this was an issue."

Teddy shrugged. "Not an issue, exactly. I mean, I'm only reviewing. I really know this stuff. But I need to be sure I don't forget any of it, and I can't stop thinking about you. That's making it hard."

Ollie forced himself not to smile. He was glad to hear that Teddy was thinking about him. He hadn't been sure for a while. Teddy was a master at hiding his emotions, and while Ollie didn't like it, he understood where that came from. Still, he wished he could break through that wall, and maybe he was. There was no other explanation for Teddy's presence here.

"Well, feel free to sit anywhere you want to."

Teddy grinned. "I will. And you, feel free to go back to work. I have stuff to do, and so do you. We can work side by side for a bit."

It was weird. Ollie wasn't used to working with people around him. He'd always worked on his own ever since he'd opened the shop, but he supposed there were worse ways to get used to having someone work along with you. He was going to have to if he wanted Cyn to work with him anyway. But the fact that this was Teddy made everything better.

Ollie went back to work. In the beginning, it was hard for him to ignore Teddy's presence, but Teddy was quiet, almost unnaturally so. Ollie could hear him breathe, and the sound of the pages of his book turning, but that was all.

Once he got used to it, it was easy to get back to work. He wasn't sure how much time passed before he finally looked up again. He was done with the bike, and he got to his feet, stretching his neck and shoulders before turning to Teddy.

He was asleep.

He'd stretched out on the couch, stomach down. One of his books was under his face, and he was using it as a pillow. It couldn't be comfortable, yet Teddy was smiling slightly.

He was adorable.

Ollie realized he probably shouldn't be thinking that about a grown man, but he couldn't help it. Teddy was a gorgeous guy, and he was Ollie's, or at least, Ollie hoped so. He wanted him to be.

And yes, Teddy *was* adorable. His cheeks were slightly pink, and his glasses were all crooked on his nose. Ollie hoped he wouldn't break them, but he was wary of trying to slip them off Teddy's face. He didn't want to wake Teddy up.

But it was time for lunch, so maybe that wouldn't be a bad idea.

Ollie went to wash off, then came back to the couch and

crouched next to it. He took a good look at Teddy, at the way his eyelashes fanned over his cheeks and slightly trembled as he slept, at the way he puffed out breaths and how he was hugging his book as if it were a pillow.

Ollie took a risk and leaned down to kiss Teddy's cheek. "Hey, sleepyhead. I thought you were here to study," he murmured.

Teddy's eyes blinked open, and he smiled sleepily. That smile went straight to Ollie's heart.

Teddy had trusted him enough to fall asleep with him close by. He'd trusted him enough to know Ollie would protect him if anything happens. Ollie had other people who trusted him, but coming from Teddy, it was important.

It was everything.

Teddy rubbed his face, or at least, he tried to. His hand collided with his glasses, though, and he scowled. Ollie chuckled and reached out to slide them off his face, folding them and putting them onto the tiny coffee table to the side.

Teddy rubbed his eyes. "Damn. I didn't mean to fall asleep."

"You haven't been sleeping well because you dream about me at night, too?" Ollie teased. He didn't expect the blush on Teddy's face, but it made him want to kiss Teddy even more. It was a feat because he always wanted to kiss Teddy.

Teddy shrugged. "I don't know. But I did tell you that I had trouble focusing, and I won't deny that you're a big part of that. I can't stop thinking about you and what we're doing."

"You mean our relationship?"

Teddy rolled his eyes. "Of course. What else?"

Ollie couldn't stop smiling. He hadn't expected his day to go this way, but he was delighted that it had. "You want some lunch?"

Teddy bit his lower lip and looked at the shop door. "Can

we wait a moment?"

"Of course." Ollie wondered what he had in mind, but he didn't have to wonder for long. Teddy reached for him as he sat up, and he wrapped his arms around Ollie's neck. Ollie almost dropped on top of him, but he managed to twist until he was falling onto the couch, settling against the hard pillows next to Teddy. Teddy laughed, and it sounded free and happy. He twisted, too, and settled against Ollie's side. Ollie didn't even think about it before wrapping his arm around his waist and holding him close.

This was perfect. This was what the future needed to look like.

Ollie looked down at Teddy. "What did you have in mind?" he asked, his voice husky. He hoped Teddy wouldn't be scared by the obvious emotions in it or in his expression.

But Teddy just smiled. He didn't run away, and he didn't try to move. He seemed to be perfectly okay with being in Ollie's arms, and Ollie wasn't going to protest. "I thought we could spend some time together before we eat," Teddy said.

"It's not the weekend," Ollie pointed out.

"I know it's not. I might not be able to focus on school, but I still know what day it is."

"I thought you only want to see me during the weekend."

"The fact that I'm here shows otherwise. I want to spend some time with you, if that's okay with you. But I can go if you have more work."

Ollie shook his head. "Stay, please." He leaned down to kiss Teddy, already smiling as he did so, but they were interrupted.

Someone cleared their throat, making Teddy jump away from Ollie.

Ollie turned around, already glaring, to find a man standing at the door, rubbing the back of his neck. "I'm sorry I interrupted, but I need to talk to Olivier."

Since this was probably a client, Ollie rose from the couch and headed toward the man, offering him his hand and not mentioning that he hated his name. How did this guy know it anyway? "You're looking for me. I'm the owner. Do you have a bike for me to look at?"

The man shook his head. "I'm not a client. I don't own a bike. But I was looking for you because I'm your father."

Ollie blinked. "I'm sorry?"

"I'm your father."

Ollie shook his head. "You can't do this. I don't care who you are, but you need to leave." Ollie couldn't face his father, not now. Maybe not ever.

Teddy had no idea what was happening. He wanted to ask, but clearly the moment wasn't right.

Ollie crossed his arms over his chest. "I told you to leave," he snapped at the man who'd just said he was his father.

Teddy tried to think about what Ollie had told him about his family. He knew Ollie had grown up with a foster family, at least during the few years before he turned eighteen. Ollie hadn't told him why, though, and Teddy hadn't asked. They were getting to know each other, but so far, they'd both skirted away from painful memories and their pasts. Teddy wished he'd asked now. He had no idea how to react in this situation, how to support Ollie.

"Please," Ollie's father said. "I'm sorry I wasn't there for you. I'm sorry I wasn't in your life. But I didn't know you existed."

Teddy sucked in a breath. Was this the first time they'd met?

"What the fuck are you talking about?" Ollie asked, his voice still harsh.

"Your mother never told me she was pregnant. I didn't

know you existed until recently, and I came here as soon as I found you."

Teddy thought this would break down Ollie's walls, but instead, Ollie shook his head. "I don't care. You weren't there for the first twenty-seven years of my life, and I don't need you for the rest of them. You know where the door is."

Ollie stomped away, toward the tiny office Teddy knew was at the back of the shop. He'd never been here, but Ollie had described the place in which he spent most of his days.

Ollie was gone, and Teddy was alone with Ollie's father.

He shuffled, wondering what he was supposed to do. He suspected Ollie would be angry with him if he talked to his father, but Ollie hadn't forbidden him to do it. What was he going to do if Teddy asked the man what was going on? Maybe someone ought to. Ollie was angry, and he wouldn't listen to his father. Teddy didn't know if whatever Ollie's father had done was forgivable, but he wouldn't find out if he didn't know what had happened.

He wanted to help. Ollie was stubborn, and he wouldn't come back. He wouldn't stop Teddy from talking to his father, though. He might not like it, but he didn't control Teddy, and Teddy wanted to help.

Ollie's father rubbed his face with both hands and sighed heavily, so heavily that Teddy could hear him from where he was on the couch. He wasn't sure Ollie's father had even noticed him.

He rose from the couch, unsure of what to do. His first instinct was to go after Ollie, of course, to make sure he was okay and ask him what was happening, but maybe he could say something to Ollie's father before going. "I'm sorry he reacted like that," Teddy finally said.

Ollie's father jumped. His eyes went wide when he looked at Teddy. "Who are you?"

He sounded rude, but Teddy didn't blame him. "I'm

Teddy. Ollie's mate."

The man's eyes widened. "My son found his mate?"

"Well, I'm here, so yes, he did. I have no idea what's going on between the two of you, but I'm sorry he treated you that way. You should leave, though."

The man looked at Teddy as if trying to read him, and it made Teddy even more nervous. "You'll take care of him?" he finally asked.

Teddy blinked. That wasn't what he'd expected. "Of course I will. He's my mate. He's a good man."

The man nodded. "I know that. I might have just found out about him, but as soon as I did, I found out everything I could. I know he hasn't had this shop long. I know he's lived with the pack since he was fifteen." His expression twisted. "I wish his mother had told me about him. I could have offered him a home when she decided to leave him."

Teddy wanted to ask what had happened, but he wanted those answers from Ollie, not from his father. "Look, I don't know what happened. I might be Ollie's mate, but we just met a few weeks ago." If even that. Teddy wasn't sure he could count the texts they'd sent each other as meeting. "But you need to give him time. It's obvious he didn't expect you to come around, and he's angry. Give him a few days to think over what your presence in his life might mean, then try to contact him again."

The man cocked his head. "That's your suggestion? To give Ollie time?"

"Yes."

"What if he ends up hating me even more after he thinks about it?"

Teddy shrugged. "Then you have to leave him alone. You're his father. I'm sure you want to be in his life, but also that you'll do everything you can to make him happy. Even if it means you never see him again."

The man scrunched his face, his entire expression morphing to grief. "You're right. Whatever happens, I want him to be happy. Even if it means I'm not in his life." He hesitated. "Tell him that, please. Tell him that I didn't know, and that if I had, I would have done everything I could to find him and to help him. And I understand if he never wants to see me again. I truly do. I just hope Ollie gives us a chance."

The man nodded at Teddy and turned around to leave. Teddy looked at him as he went, wondering what the fuck he was supposed to do now.

He was supposed to be on Ollie's side, and he was. But from the little Teddy knew about the situation, this man hadn't even known Ollie existed until recently. That was why he hadn't been able to help Ollie while he was growing up. Ollie was angry, and that was understandable, but would he be able to let go of his anger to see the situation for what it was?

Teddy hoped so.

Once Ollie's father had left, Teddy turned around to follow Ollie into the office. He wasn't surprised to see Ollie behind his desk, his body folded in the cramped space against the wall. His elbows were on the desk, his face buried in his hands.

Teddy bit his lower lip. "Ollie?"

Ollie didn't look up. "Is he gone?"

"He is. Do you want to talk about it?"

Teddy held his breath. He wasn't surprised when Ollie shook his head, and that left him at a loss. He didn't know what to do. He wasn't the best person to comfort someone when they were grieving, and that was obviously what Ollie was doing. Teddy wasn't sure what he could do, if there was anything that he could do to help Ollie, but since his first instinct was to go to his mate and comfort him, that was what he did. He stepped closer to the desk, sliding into the space between it and the wall to put himself next to Ollie, then he hugged Ollie's upper body, wrapping his arms around him and holding him close.

He felt Ollie tense, and for a few seconds, he expected his mate to push him away. Then Ollie relaxed, his body going slack against Teddy's as he leaned against him.

This wasn't what Teddy had expected from their relationship. It was terrifying to be able to comfort someone this way because it meant it was important to Ollie. It meant Ollie would do the same for him if their roles were reversed.

"I know you said you don't want to talk about it," Teddy said. "But I'm here if you do. I don't know your past, not yet. I can tell it's painful, though, and I need you to know that while I might not have been through the same thing as you did, my life hasn't been easy. Well, it wasn't easy until I was thirteen and my brother took me home. But I know what it's like to lose a parent. Hell, I lost both of them, although I've never known my father. But yeah. I get how hard dealing with this can be. So I'm here for you if you need me, but I won't push."

Teddy wasn't sure what else he could do. Teddy wanted to know what Ollie was hiding, he wanted to tell him that if *he* had the possibility of having a relationship with his parents, he would take it. But he wasn't Ollie, and Ollie wasn't him, so this would have to do for now.

Ollie was surprised but relieved to have Teddy here with him. He hadn't been sure how Teddy would react to what had just happened. Hell, he wasn't sure how *he* was reacting.

He'd never expected his father to walk into his shop. Never in his life would have thought he'd meet the man. He'd known about him for years—his mother might not have told his father about Ollie, but she had told Ollie about the man she'd had sex with. It had been more details than Ollie ever wanted, but he'd gotten a name out of her, and he'd done some research. He'd been tempted to reach out, but he'd thought that since his father couldn't be bothered to be a part of his life, neither should Ollie.

But Ollie's father hadn't known.

Ollie leaned harder against Teddy and took a deep breath. He wanted to doubt the man's word. He wanted to be sure that it had been a lie, but he couldn't be. He knew his mother, and she was more than capable of doing something like that. She probably wouldn't even realize how wrong it had been not to tell Ollie's father about his existence. She was that way, and nothing Ollie said or did would ever change her, which was why he kept his distance now that he could.

Teddy's hand ran through Ollie's hair, and he gently pulled. He'd told Ollie that he didn't have to talk if he didn't want to, and he didn't, but Teddy deserved to know.

If Ollie's father had found him, had come to visit him, that meant he had a reason to. Ollie doubted the man would just disappear from his life again, and there was a good chance that Teddy would be there next time, too.

Ollie swallowed and leaned away. Teddy didn't move far, sitting on the edge of the desk and taking one of Ollie's hands to twine their fingers together. He nodded encouragingly, but Ollie had to look away to tell him about his life.

"My mom has always been *weird*, I guess is the best word to describe her. She's flighty. She never stays in the same place for long, can't keep a job, things like that. I guess some people would call her a free spirit, but I call her mom. She dragged me around the country, from town to town, and we lived in motels or with her boyfriends. I realize I'm lucky none of them abused me or anything."

This was hard, much harder than Ollie had thought it would be. He'd come to terms with his past and his parents, or at least, he'd thought he had. But now he was forced to face all of this again, and he didn't know how he would deal with it, or if he could.

"When I was fifteen, we came here to Gillham. I didn't usually go to school much. Most of the time, she simply forgot that I needed to go, and I wasn't the most responsible teenager. But someone noticed me in town. They noticed me, and they realized I didn't have a good family life." Ollie snorted softly. "Or a family life, period. My mother has never actually been a mother to me. So when Kameron came to talk to her and offered her to leave me with them, she agreed. I think she was relieved that she'd be able to live her life the way she wanted to without having to drag me around."

"I'm so sorry," Teddy murmured.

Ollie was grateful to have his mate by his side, but he didn't want to see the pity in Teddy's eyes. He knew that Teddy had gone through a lot, too. He'd lost his mother, and she'd been a real mom to him. That had to have hurt even more than what Ollie had gone through.

Ollie shrugged. "It's fine. In the beginning, I was pissed. She was the only thing I'd ever known, and I didn't want to stay here with strangers. I was terrified. But she never looked back. She didn't even think twice about it. She dumped me with the pack and left town, and I didn't have a choice." Ollie chuckled at the memories. "Not that I didn't try. I ran away once, but with all the shifters around here, they found me easily."

"And you've been living with the pack ever since."

"I have. You know they put me with a foster family. Mary Jane and Bill had three sons of their own, but they were all grown up by the time I got here. That was why they agreed to take on foster kids. I wasn't the only one. I stayed with them for the next three years and grew close to Gabriel, who was one of my foster brothers. He's a few years older than me, but we're still close. The pack helped me finish high school, then everything else. Thanks to the pack, I learned to do this job, and when I decided I wanted to open my own shop, the pack helped me once more. This has become my family, even though my mother is still around somewhere. Sometimes, she calls me or even comes into town to see me. She usually wants money."

Ollie finally looked at Teddy. There *was* the pity he'd expected in his eyes, but also a fierce affection, and that, Ollie hadn't expected. He knew Teddy was starting to care about him, just like he was starting to care about Teddy, but even though they were mates, they were still tiptoeing around each other.

"She sounds . . ." Teddy started, but he didn't seem to be able to find a way to finish that.

"She does," Ollie agreed. "So don't be surprised if you see her around sometime."

Teddy hesitated, then asked, "What about your father?"

Ollie shook his head. "I've always known who he was. My mother didn't hide that from me. She told me how they met, and about the time they spent together. I know she only found out she was pregnant with me after she left him, but I thought she told him about it. I thought he didn't care, and that he didn't want anything to do with me. I thought that he was the reason I was in the situation I was in. Even though for the first fifteen years of my life, my mother was the only parent I knew, I realized she wasn't the best mother. But she was mine, and I didn't want to lose her. I thought it was my father's fault that we had to live the way we did. And when my mother left me here, I blamed him, too."

"Do you still blame him?"

Ollie wasn't sure how to answer that. "I'm an adult now. I know that none of this was his fault."

"That doesn't mean you don't blame him anymore. Blame

isn't logical most of the time. You were hurt a lot when you were a kid, and that's bound to leave traces, even now that you're older."

"I know it wasn't his fault, especially if my mother never told him about me. But I don't know if I can forgive him anyway. He was never a part of my life. I thought he didn't want to be."

"But maybe he does." Teddy's voice was soft. "That's why he was here, isn't it? You didn't give him time to explain, but he did say that he just found out about you recently. And what did he do when he did? He came to find you. He came to talk to you."

"I know. I'm just not sure it will be enough. I have so much resentment toward him that I don't know if I can even talk to him."

Teddy nodded. "I understand that, and of course, I won't push you into doing something you're not comfortable with. But take it from me. I lost my father when I was a baby. I never knew him. Then I lost my mother when I was a teenager, just a few years younger than you were when your mother left you here. We both grew up with broken families, but now, you have a chance at having a father. I understand it's not going to be easy, and you have every right to push him away, and not to want anything to do with him. But don't dismiss him just because of something your mother did. It wouldn't be fair to him or to you."

Ollie raised Teddy's hand and kissed the back of it in a gesture that was quickly becoming one of his favorites. He loved seeing Teddy's cheeks flushed in pleasure and slight embarrassment. "I get what you're saying," he agreed.

"But you're not sure what you're going to do."

"I'm not. I want to give him a chance, especially if what he's saying is true. Because you're right. I have a chance to be with my father. It's not something I'd ever thought possible, and now it is. But there is a lot between us, and most of it, I don't have power over. I can't change the way I think or the way I feel." Ollie hated this. He'd come to terms with his mother's behavior a long time ago. He'd accepted that she would never be a mother to him. But to find out that she never even bothered to tell his father he was alive? That was a betrayal that hurt more than when she left him here.

Ollie didn't know if he could deal with this. He didn't know what the future would look like, not when it came to his father.

But he did know that Teddy wasn't going anywhere. It would have been so easy for him to go, but he was still here. He was still here, and he was supporting Ollie when no one else was.

Ollie looked at his mate. "Will you stay here? With me?"

Teddy blinked. "What do you mean?"

"I want to spend the night with you." Ollie knew it was a huge step for both of them. "I'm not saying we have to do anything. I just don't want to be alone today."

Teddy smiled. "Of course. I'll do everything I can to make you feel okay." His smile turned wicked. "And to be honest, I wouldn't mind if we did *something*."

Ollie laughed. He still didn't know what would happen with his family — if he could call what he had a family — but he did know that he would have Teddy at the end of the day, and tomorrow.

That was enough for now.

CHAPTER SIX

Teddy was falling in love with Ollie.

It wasn't a bad thing. If he forced himself to stop panicking and think with his heart, he knew that. He needed to use his brain because he knew that part of his anatomy worked well.

But his brain wasn't the organ involved in this, was it? Or maybe it was. Teddy didn't know how falling in love worked, but he was pretty sure the heart didn't actually have anything to do with it. Not that it mattered. What *did* matter was the fact that he was falling in love with Ollie, and he wasn't sure what to do about it.

Was there anything he should do?

He'd been spending a lot of his days with Ollie, either at the shop or at his apartment. He'd stopped wondering what that meant because he knew. He was lucky no one was asking questions, but he knew they were coming. Only a handful of people knew that he and Ollie were mates for now, but Nysys had already been sticking his nose into Teddy's business since Teddy was spending so much time away from home, and he wouldn't stop until he had his answers. Teddy didn't want to give them to him yet.

He already knew what Nysys would do once he found out Teddy and Ollie were mates. He'd start asking even more questions, and he might try to organize yet another party, this time for them. Teddy knew he should be happy that his family was over the moon for him, and he was. He didn't want to think about what a party with the entire pride there would entail.

It wasn't like he and Ollie were getting married. They hadn't even talked about bonding yet, and even though Teddy knew it was something he would want to do eventually, he didn't think he and Ollie were anywhere near close to being ready for that.

Besides, Teddy wasn't the only one involved. Ollie was, too, and he'd been behaving strangely since his father had tried coming back into his life. Teddy didn't know what to do about it, or if there was anything that he could do at all. He wanted to help Ollie. Ollie hadn't asked him to, though. It was obvious he wanted Teddy to stay close and be there for him, and that was what Teddy was doing. But he couldn't help but wonder if he should be doing *more*.

Maybe he should talk to someone who was already mated, or at the very least, who had met their mates. The problem was that apart from his brother, he didn't know a lot of people. Sterling and Adam came to mind, but they weren't friends. Teddy felt self-conscious and embarrassed just thinking about asking them for advice, especially about something so private and personal.

So that left his brother, and that was an entirely different kind of embarrassment. Jayden would answer any questions Teddy had for him, of course. He'd probably be flustered and would babble like crazy, but it wasn't anything Teddy wasn't used to. Of course, it wasn't like Teddy *needed* advice. He wanted to talk to someone, but he already knew what was happening, even though he had no idea what the next step was.

His relationship with Ollie still felt fragile, and Teddy didn't want to risk it, especially since he'd been the one trying to keep as much distance as possible between them until now. He still wanted to graduate. He still wanted to focus on his studies. But he'd found that spending time with Ollie wasn't as distracting as he's he'd expected it to be.

Now that Teddy had accepted that Ollie wasn't going anywhere, it was easier to deal with everything. He and Ollie had been spending time together in the evenings, and they'd been sharing a bed, with all that entailed. Well, almost all it entailed, but Teddy didn't want to think about that right now. What he *did* want to think about was that now that he knew Ollie, he was able to focus on his books more when he needed to because he knew he'd have Ollie soon. He was confident that he could finish his degree with high grades, and he would.

But he also had other things to focus on now, mainly Ollie and the way he was behaving.

"Something is going on with you."

Teddy jerked so hard that he almost knocked his coffee off the table. He blinked, only half surprised to see Sterling standing by his tiny table at the coffee shop, looking down at him. "I'm sorry?" he asked.

Sterling wrinkled his nose. He was holding a cup of steaming coffee, and to Teddy's surprise, he sat on the other side of the table. Teddy hadn't asked him to, and he wasn't about to tell Sterling he needed to leave, but he wondered what was happening.

Sterling leaned forward. "Is it something with Ollie?"

Teddy wasn't going to blush, or at least, he hoped he wouldn't. He certainly didn't want to show Sterling how embarrassed he was. "I'm studying."

Sterling arched a brow. "Well, I do see the open book, but I don't think you were looking at it. I think you were lost in your thoughts."

Teddy was pretty sure he was blushing by now, but he focused on Sterling. "All right. Maybe I'm a little distracted."

Sterling nodded, satisfied, and leaned back in his chair. He took a sip of coffee while staring at Teddy, and Teddy squirmed in his chair.

He wasn't used to this. He wasn't used to having friends. He didn't know how to behave, which was one of the reasons he usually stayed away from people. He was socially awkward, and the fact that he'd forced himself to focus on high school, then college and university, probably had a lot to do with that. He'd never let himself learn how to be with others socially, and he was paying the price right now.

Sterling huffed. "Okay, so you're not going to tell me what's going on if I don't try to get it out of you."

Teddy sighed. "Why do you want to know?"

"I've been seeing you around a lot these days," Sterling said instead of answering. "Are you moving in with Ollie?"

Teddy shook his head, but he was spending most of his time here, including the nights, and he'd filled several drawers with his things in Ollie's bedroom. They might not have had *the talk*, but for all intents and purposes, Teddy *was* living with Ollie.

Sterling tapped his fingertips on the table. "Okay, since you don't want to talk, I'm going to try guessing, okay?"

Teddy wanted to say no, but he found himself nodding instead. He'd just been thinking he needed someone to talk to, and he still did.

Sterling never looked away from Teddy as he spoke. "Okay. So you and Ollie are living together. You're moving to Gillham, and that's good. But you're worried about something. What is it? You don't have a job in Whitedell, do you?"

"I don't." Not that Teddy hadn't wanted one, but both Jayden and Dominic, the Whitedell pride alpha, had convinced him to focus on school. He knew he was privileged, which was one more reason for him to graduate with high grades.

"So it's not that. And I don't think it's school, either. I mean, you can get a Nix to shimmer you around just as easily as any of us. Maybe your family? I thought your brother had accepted your relationship with Ollie."

Teddy sighed again. He didn't like this game. "Yes, Jayden is happy for me, and so is his mate. And he doesn't care that I'll probably end up moving to Gillham. Like you said, it's fairly easy to shimmer here, and he lives halfway between here and Whitedell anyway. He's not going to be a problem."

"What is, then?"

Teddy swallowed. "I'm not sure." He didn't want to tell Sterling about Ollie's father. He doubted Ollie would want anyone to know about the man. "I'm just not sure how to do this whole relationship thing. I've never had one, not a serious one anyway." Teddy didn't count his few high school boyfriends as relationships. The longest he'd been with someone back then had been a few months, and that was nothing similar to what he had with Ollie.

"You'll learn. We all do. I mean, you're what? Twenty-five? Twenty-six?"

Teddy frowned. "Twenty-six. What does that have to do with anything?"

"Nothing, except that you have plenty of years to learn. And you'll learn with the best man possible since Ollie is your mate." He hesitated. "But if you want some advice, talk to him. Talking with your mate will always help. I've had to learn that the hard way. Adam came into my life at the hardest moment possible, and it was easy to think it would be better to withdraw and focus on my siblings. I needed his help, though, and his support. And while it's still hard to talk sometimes because I feel weird about talking to anyone about how I feel, it does make things easier. We're a couple, and so are you and Ollie. I'm not telling you to babble everything to him, including what you're buying him for Christmas or whatever, but important things? Those are things you need to decide together. That means you need to talk to him. It's one of the trickiest things to learn in a relationship, but also one of the most important."

This was exactly the kind of advice Teddy had yearned for, and now he had it.

He didn't know how sound it was, but it wasn't like he had other ideas. He knew that the reason Ollie was a bit cold and standoffish was because of his father. There was no other reason for him to behave like that.

Or at least, Teddy hoped so. He wasn't sure what he would do if it was something else, and he didn't want to think about it, not yet.

Possibly, not ever.

Ollie wasn't surprised when his phone rang again. He'd been fielding phone calls from his father ever since the man had entered his shop that day, and he still hadn't answered. He was tempted not to. He didn't *want* to. He had no idea what his father wanted from him, and he didn't want to find out. The thought was terrifying.

Maybe he should have asked what his father wanted that day, and then he would have been done with it. Instead, he was still here, wondering why the fuck a man he'd never met in his life wanted to talk to him so badly.

The worst was the hope. Ollie wasn't sure where it came from. He'd never wanted to meet his father. He'd never hoped to get anything from the man. Of course, that was mostly because his mother had lied to him, or rather, because he'd thought his father knew about him just like he knew about his father.

Ollie had a hard time believing his father hadn't known about him, but it fit with what he knew about his mother. He didn't know if she'd done it on purpose, if she hadn't told him that Ollie existed because she hadn't wanted him in their life, but it was possible. Anything was possible with Ollie's mother. He wouldn't put it past her to forget to tell his father she was pregnant or that she'd had the baby. She didn't care about people except for herself, and that included Ollie.

But that left Ollie in this situation. He wasn't sure what to do. He wanted to ask his father what had happened, how it was possible that he hadn't known. He was also curious. Ollie's mother was a human, and that meant his father was the shifter. It probably meant that the man was a hedgehog shifter like Ollie, but Ollie had never met a hedgehog shifter before. He didn't think it mattered, but still, knowing there was another one out there, one related to him, made him feel less alone.

He rubbed his face. Having his father in his life, even though it had only been for a few minutes, had turned him into a mess. He didn't know what to think or how to feel. He didn't know what to do. He hated it, mostly because being overwhelmed meant he'd been pushing Teddy away, too. Teddy hadn't said anything about it, bless him, but Ollie knew he had to have noticed. Maybe that made it easier for him to focus on his studies, but Ollie didn't like it.

He and Teddy were just starting their relationship. They were moving fast, but that didn't mean they shouldn't move carefully. They were already living together, even though they hadn't had the talk, and Ollie wanted that to continue. That meant he should probably sit down with Teddy and have a chat with him, but it was hard to think about anything that wasn't his father when the man kept calling him. Teddy deserved better, though. Ollie had promised him he would be better than this, and he needed things to change. He didn't want Teddy to regret giving him this chance. He never wanted that to happen.

A hesitant knock on his open office door made Ollie look up. He wasn't surprised to see Teddy there, and he also wasn't surprised to see that Teddy wasn't sure whether to enter or not. Ollie hated that, and his heart squeezed painfully in his chest.

He put his phone down and waved at Teddy to come in. "What are you doing here? I thought you went to the coffee shop to study."

Teddy shrugged. He dumped his backpack onto one of the empty chairs on the other side of Ollie's desk, then hesitated again. Ollie knew he wasn't sure whether to sit down or to walk around the desk to come to him. Ollie knew which one he'd prefer, but he stayed silent. Teddy was the one who should make this decision.

"I was at the coffee shop, but it wasn't as easy to focus as I hoped it would be."

Ollie couldn't help but smile at that. "Do I still distract you even if I'm not there?"

Teddy's eyes narrowed. "Damn right, you do. But it's not because you're my mate or because we're in a relationship. It's because you've been acting weird."

Ollie sighed. "I'm sorry. I never meant to distract you or make you worried."

Teddy's expression softened. "I know that, and I know that the way you've been behaving is related to your father. That's why I haven't pushed. I don't want you to feel forced to talk to me, but I do wish you'd say something, if not to me, to Gabriel, or your foster parents. To anyone, really. It's obvious something is going on with you, and I want to help you, but I don't know how."

Ollie wasn't sure anyone could help him, to be honest. He wasn't sure there was anything anyone could do.

He decided to pour his heart out to Teddy. Who better than him? "I told you about my mother."

Teddy nodded. "You did. Has she contacted you?"

Ollie shook his head. "I haven't told her about this. I don't want her to come here, especially not now." Ollie's relationship with his mother was weird. He loved her, but she'd never been a mother, especially in the past ten years. Most days, Ollie didn't think about her. He didn't call her. She came to visit every so often, but it was usually when she needed something, and she didn't even see how wrong that was. "I want to hear her side of the story, but I don't think I'm ready for it."

Teddy slowly nodded. "That's understandable. Are you still avoiding your father?"

Ollie gently snorted. "You already know me so well."

"It's more that I've seen you doing it ever since the man came in to talk to you. I know he's been calling, too. You haven't been answering."

"I don't know *what* to say." Ollie was utterly lost, and he didn't know if there was a way out of the situation. "I want to talk to him. I want to hear his side of the story. I'm curious about him, especially now that he told me he didn't know about me."

"So why don't you answer his phone calls? You don't even have to see him if you don't feel ready for that. Just answer your phone, tell him you're not ready, and I'm sure he'll wait. If he wants a relationship with you and to be your father, he'll do it."

"What if he doesn't?" Ollie asked, and he hated how weak his voice sounded.

Teddy's expression twisted, and Ollie prayed he wasn't pitying him. He didn't want his mate to feel that for him, ever.

"I just mean that he might not want me in his life," Ollie continued. "He might want to see me, or something like that. Maybe he wants to find out about my mother. Maybe he's still in love with her and wants to find her."

Teddy shook his head. "I doubt that's it. You didn't talk to him because you left as soon as he explained who he was, but I did."

Ollie straightened in his chair. That was right. He'd forgotten about that because he'd been busy worrying about his parents. "You talked to him?"

"I did. I wasn't sure if you wanted me to or if you'd be angry, so I didn't mention it. And it wasn't a full conversation, to be honest. But he asked me what he could do to get you to talk to him. He asked me what to do since I'm your mate."

"And what did you tell him?"

"To give you time. I think that's what you needed, and that you're finally ready to face the situation. You don't have to if you don't want to, of course, but I do think you should talk to him. It's the only way you'll get answers to your questions, and the only way you have to get to know him. You don't have to have a relationship with him if you realize that you don't want one, but I think you should give him and yourself a chance. You deserve your father. Besides, it's not like your father wanted to abandon you. He didn't know you existed, and now that he does, he wants to meet you. I think that's a good thing, but of course, you're the one in charge in this situation. You're the one who will make decisions. I can only advise you and tell you what I would do in your place, but I can't do it for you, and I want you to think well about this. Meeting your father has the possibility of changing your life. I know you already have a family with Mary Jane and Bill, and that's good. It won't ever change. But you have a chance at something more, and I wish I had that with my parents."

Ollie felt guilty. While he'd been obsessing over whether or not to answer his phone and talk to his father, Teddy would never have that. He'd never known his father, and the man was dead. He'd lost his mother when he was a teenager. He only had his brother and the Whitedell pride. It was better than nothing, but they couldn't replace parents. "I'll talk to him."

Teddy's smile was soft and gentle. "Good. You deserve a

family. You deserve people who love you, as many as possible."

Ollie wanted to tell him he already had them, but he didn't. What Teddy had said was true—Ollie had his foster family, Gabriel, and even other pack members, but it wasn't the same. Ollie had already been fifteen when he'd arrived, and even though Mary Jane and Bill were his foster parents and the only *real* parents he'd known, he'd only been with them for a few years.

Meeting his father wouldn't change how much he loved them, but he was curious about where he'd come from.

And now, he had the chance to find out. He just needed to take it.

Teddy wasn't surprised when Ollie answered his phone the next time it rang and his father readily agreed to meet him. He'd expected it. He knew the man wanted to meet his son, so it made sense, and he hoped he wasn't wrong. He thought that Ollie's father wanted to be a father to him, as much as that was possible, considering Ollie was twenty-seven. He hoped that Ollie would give the man a chance. There was no way Ollie's father could make amends if Ollie didn't let him.

Not that Ollie needed to. His father would have had to make amends if he'd avoided his son up until now, but he hadn't known about Ollie's existence. That wasn't Ollie's fault, but it wasn't his father's, either. No, that fault rested on the shoulders of Ollie's mother, and if Teddy ever met her, he'd make sure to tell her what he thought about that.

From what Ollie had told him, he knew she'd never been a real mother, and he hated that. Even though he'd lost his mom when he was thirteen, he knew what it felt like to be loved by her. She'd been there for the first part of his life, and he'd always be grateful for that. He'd always have the memories, too, which was more than Ollie could say.

Ollie had his foster family, and having his father in his life wouldn't change that. But Teddy could see how much Ollie yearned to meet the man, to talk to him, and he prayed that things would go the way Ollie wanted them to. He wasn't sure what way that was yet, but he suspected that even though Ollie was doing his best to keep some distance between himself and his father, he wanted a relationship with him.

Teddy understood that. His father was dead, but if he'd been alive, he would have wanted to meet him, too. He'd never have the chance, but Ollie did, and Teddy was glad he was taking it.

Teddy did his best not to listen to the phone call, but he couldn't avoid it, not while he stayed in the office. He looked around instead of staring at Ollie, though, thinking about school, his brother, and whatever else crossed his mind while he wasn't listening.

"Teddy?"

Teddy startled. He'd been doing a good job of not listening in, apparently. "Yes?"

Ollie chuckled. He was looking at Teddy, his eyes wide and his cheeks slightly flushed. "He wants to meet me now."

"I know. I heard."

"He said he stuck around in the hope that I would want to talk to him."

That meant a lot to Ollie. Teddy could see it. "And you agreed to meet him?"

"I did. I want to talk to him. He said he's at the coffee shop right now, and that we should head that way."

Ollie's father had obviously come in after Teddy had left. Teddy was relieved. He wasn't sure what he would have done if he'd had to face the man. It depended on what kind of person Ollie's father was, and Teddy hoped he wouldn't have pushed to talk to Teddy since Ollie wouldn't speak to him. But there was only one way to find out, and that was by getting to know the man.

Teddy nodded and rose from his chair. "I'll head home, then," he said, reaching for his backpack.

"Can you come with me?"

Teddy was only half surprised that Ollie was asking. He turned to face his mate, trying to read his expression. "Are you sure you don't want privacy?"

Ollie shook his head. "I'm going to tell you everything that happens anyway. I need your support more than privacy."

Teddy wasn't sure about that. He wasn't sure Ollie's father would be comfortable with having him there, but he couldn't say no to Ollie. Ollie was his mate, and that was more important than a stranger's comfort. "Of course I'll come with you. Shall we head there, then?"

Ollie nodded and rose from his chair. "Let's go."

Teddy followed him out of the office. They didn't know each other well yet, but he wouldn't back down from this, even though he didn't know what would happen, or maybe because of that.

Ollie was trusting Teddy with the situation, and Teddy wanted to be there for him. He didn't think Ollie would have asked anyone else to be present during this meeting, not even Gabriel, and that made Teddy's stomach churn in a pleasant way. Ollie wanted Teddy in his life, and Teddy wanted that, too. He never wanted to leave, and he almost couldn't believe how much things had changed over such a short amount of time. He'd gone from being terrified that he wouldn't be able to graduate because of Ollie to living with him. He still didn't know what would happen with school, but he was certain he could graduate with good grades. Once that was done, he'd find a job.

In Gillham.

There was no denying that he wouldn't go back to Whitedell. He might still have some things there, but he couldn't even remember the last time he'd been at the mansion—probably when he needed clean underwear or something. Everything had changed, and it would continue to. Now Ollie was meeting his father, and he would need Teddy's support. That would bring them together even more so, and it was one more step forward in their relationship.

Teddy didn't know what the future held for them, but he knew he wanted Ollie.

"Thanks for doing this," Ollie murmured.

Teddy smiled at him. "Any time. And I know you would do the same for me."

"Of course I would. But I know that while we're together, we're not bonded. It would be easy for you to step out of the situation. I can only imagine how you feel, but I'm glad you agreed to come with me."

Teddy snatched Ollie's hand and linked their fingers together. "How I feel? How I feel is worried about you. I want to be there for you and to shield you from whatever pain might come your way. I'm praying your father wants to get to know you and to be in your life, but neither of us can know that, and I'm terrified you're going to be hurt by the situation, and that I'll have pushed you into something you shouldn't have done."

Ollie frowned. "But even if he hurts me, it wouldn't be your fault. It would be his. Surely, you know that."

"I do. But our relationship is very new, and your father just entered your life. I can't help but wonder if you're going to link those two events in your mind, even if unwillingly. You're taking my advice and talking to him. What happens if he's an asshole? What happens if he wants something from you, and just that thing?" Ollie had mentioned his mother coming around for money, and Teddy couldn't help but wonder if that was what they were looking at with Ollie's father. He hoped not, but they wouldn't know until they talked to him.

To Teddy's surprise, Ollie shrugged. "That won't be any different from what my mother wants. She's my mother, and I grew up with her, but she's never been a mom. I wouldn't be surprised if my father did the same, and I won't be hurt."

But Teddy knew that wasn't the case. How could Ollie not be hurt by his parents only wanting money from him? It should be the other way around. They should be the ones present for Ollie if he needed them, be it for money or anything else.

Ollie and Teddy had messed up relationships with their families. Teddy didn't have one to talk about, except for Jayden, and Ollie's was a mess.

But they had each other. That had to count for something, right? Teddy hoped it did. He wanted so much more than what they had, and he knew he could have it. It was just there, in reach. Now wasn't the time to talk about it, but eventually, they would, and Teddy already knew what his answer to that question would be.

It might sound ridiculous, and it might be rushed, but he didn't care. Even though he and Ollie were young and they'd just met, even though all his attention had been on his studies up until now, he wanted to bond with Ollie. He'd never wanted something more, not even to graduate and make Jayden proud.

He wasn't quite sure how to deal with that, but he didn't think it mattered. Things would settle down eventually, and if they didn't, then he'd talk to Ollie. But it would have to wait. Teddy wasn't the center of the situation. This was all about Ollie, and hopefully, everything would go well.

Ollie was glad Teddy was coming with him. He wasn't sure he would have had the courage to walk into the coffee shop otherwise.

He didn't know when Teddy had become so central in his life, and he didn't care. He and Teddy had been spending so much time together. Their lives were already twining, becoming one. They were mates, so that had been bound to happen sooner or later, but he was glad it happened now. He wasn't sure what he would have done if he'd have had to face his father on his own. He didn't want to think about that, either. What would have happened didn't matter, not when it wouldn't happen. Teddy wasn't going anywhere. He would be next to Ollie every step of the way, and that was what Ollie needed.

They stepped into the coffee shop and looked around. Ollie didn't think he would ever forget how his father looked, even though he'd seen him only a few minutes. He wasn't surprised to see him in the corner of the room, alone at a small table, but he *was* surprised when he noticed the signs that his father was nervous.

The man was bouncing his knee. He was also tapping his fingertips on the table, and he kept looking around. That was how he noticed Ollie as soon as he walked in, and he jerked from his chair, almost tilting it to the floor. He managed to grab it, and his cheeks flushed.

That wasn't what Ollie had expected. He wasn't sure what he thought would happen exactly, but not this. His father was nervous, and he didn't understand why.

"You can do this," Teddy murmured, leaning closer to Ollie.

"I know." And Ollie did. Seeing his father so eager and nervous to meet him made it easier to step toward him. He hadn't wanted to think about why his father wanted to meet him, but he thought that maybe it would be something like his mother. He didn't think so anymore, though, even if his father needed money. Ollie didn't think he did—he was *happy* to see Ollie, or at least, Ollie thought so.

Ollie and Teddy headed toward the counter to grab coffee. Ollie didn't really want anything to drink, but he thought it would be useful for him to have something to keep his hands occupied. He was used to that, since he worked with his hands every day, and spending time at the counter getting coffee meant less time having to look his father in the eyes. He needed these few minutes to gather his thoughts, to breathe in and out, and try to calm himself. Teddy's presence with him was helping, but it wasn't working totally. Ollie hadn't expected it to, but he wished he felt calmer.

He and Teddy headed toward the table as soon as they got their coffee, and they settled on the other side of it. Ollie's father was staring, and it made Ollie want to wriggle in his seat. Instead, Ollie focused on his coffee, taking a few sips.

"Olivier. I'm so happy to see you," Ollie's father said, and Ollie realized he didn't even know the man's name, not for sure. He couldn't believe anything his mother had said.

He cleared his throat, wondering how to ask that without sounding rude. He supposed he would sound rude either way. His mother had told him about the man she had sex with, but she'd never gone into details. Ollie had never asked because if his father couldn't be bothered to have Ollie in his life, then Ollie didn't want anything to do with him. He'd been wrong, though, and now, he needed to fix that.

"I wasn't sure you'd come," Ollie's father continued.

Ollie nodded. "I get it. I wasn't sure I'd come, either. And it's Ollie, or Oliver, please. I hate my name." Probably because it reminded him of his mother's French origin, but Ollie had never analyzed that. It didn't matter.

He bit his lower lip. "If you don't mind me asking, what's your name?"

The man's expression twisted with pain, and Ollie felt guilty. This was Ollie's mother's fault, and he couldn't help but hate her right now. The next time he saw her, he was going to tell her what he thought about what she'd done. She probably wouldn't care, but at least, it would be out there. Maybe it was time for Ollie to cut ties with her. He'd kept his relationship with her because he didn't want to lose her, but perhaps it would be better. He didn't need that kind of negativity in his life, especially not now that he'd found Teddy.

"Of course. My name is Mark."

Ollie snorted. "Well, she was close. She told me you were Marcus. It's a pleasure to meet you." Ollie extended his hand, and Mark shook it.

"Is it?" he asked.

Ollie couldn't help but smile. "I won't deny it's weird. I never expected this to happen, but then, I also never expected to meet Teddy, yet here we are."

Mark smiled. "He told me he's your mate."

Ollie squeezed his hand, turning to smile at him. "He is. We only met recently, but we're already living together." Even though they'd never talked about it, Ollie never wanted Teddy to leave.

Teddy's cheeks flushed, and he pushed his glasses up his nose. "But we're not here to talk about Ollie and me," he told Mark. "I'm glad you reached out, and that you gave Ollie time to think about this."

Mark nodded at him. "And I'm glad I followed your advice. I wasn't sure it was sound, but you were right. Ollie needed time." He turned his attention back to Ollie. "I want to apologize. I would've done that the other day, but I didn't think you would have listened. I'm sorry about not being in your life until now. I swear to you, I had no idea you existed."

Ollie believed him. "Can you tell me what happened?" He wanted to hear it. He knew it probably wouldn't look good for his mother, but it didn't matter. He was done protecting her, especially since she hadn't protected him so many years ago.

Mark nodded and leaned back in his chair. He wrapped both hands around his cup of coffee, and his gaze became distant. "I met Lacey almost, God, thirty years ago. I already knew she wasn't the kind of girl to settle down, so I didn't keep my hopes up, but I really liked her. We had fun together, I guess you could say. I won't go into details, of course, but if she'd wanted to, I would've been ready to marry her or to take care of you. But she never gave me a chance. We were together for a month, maybe a little more, then she just disappeared. I tried to find her. I thought something had happened to her in the beginning, but then a friend told me he'd seen her with someone else, leaving town, and I realized that she'd just skipped town. She never planned to stay with me, and while I would have appreciated being warned when she decided to leave, I was okay with that. But I had no idea she was pregnant with you."

"I don't think she knew, either," Ollie said. "She told me about that part of her life. She never changed, you know? She told me she met my father, and that you were together for a bit. She never went into details either, and I decided to stay away from you, so I didn't ask."

Mark blinked. "But you didn't know my name."

"I thought I did. Marcus is close enough to Mark, and I had an address." Ollie couldn't help but smile. "Your parents' house, I think."

Mark's eyes widened. "My mother's now. My father died several years ago."

Ollie nodded. "My mother told me she met your parents once. That's how she knew the place."

"And you got that from her? Even though you weren't planning on reaching out?"

"I'm sorry I didn't know, but that's how things were. I was convinced you didn't want anything to do with me."

"But you were curious enough to find out where I lived."

"It's not like I kept tabs on you. But yes, I wanted to know where you were just in case I needed to find you one day. That address was more than enough for me. It's why I never reached out." And now Ollie regretted it. He couldn't be sure his father was honest when he said that he'd never known about him, but he suspected he was. That meant that Ollie had wasted almost ten years, and he wasn't sure how to feel about that.

Teddy squeezed his hand and brought Ollie back to the present.

"I can't tell you how guilty I feel about you growing up without a father or a family," Mark continued.

"I won't deny things have been hard. Then my mother left me here when I was fifteen, and things got better for me. I spent the next few years with a foster family. They're *still* my family. We're very close."

"I'm happy you had someone."

That was yet another clue that Mark was serious. He wanted Ollie to be happy, even if it meant that he didn't consider him his father. "They're good people, and I was safe and happy. I still am. They're the reason I have my own shop and an apartment. I don't know where I would be if my mother hadn't left me here." And he didn't want to think about it. It was too easy to imagine how Ollie would have ended up if his mother had continued dragging him around the country.

He had his father now, even though he didn't know what it would mean for him. He was going to try, though. He was still somewhat angry and resentful, but he believed his father hadn't had anything to do with this and that he hadn't known about him. They had time to get to know each other, and that was what Ollie wanted right now.

He didn't know if meeting Mark had anything to do with meeting Teddy, but he suspected it did. He didn't know if he would have listened to Mark if Teddy hadn't pushed him to, and that meant that the main reason he would get to know his father was his mate.

Teddy had arrived in Ollie's life just at the right moment, and Ollie loved him for it.

CHAPTER SEVEN

Feeling Ollie inside him was heaven, or at least it was what heaven should feel like. He didn't have a lot to compare it to, but this was the best sex he'd ever had, hands down.

The fact that it was with Ollie probably had a lot to do with that, but Teddy wasn't thinking about how good Ollie was at this, even though he was. There was more to it than just the physical aspect, and as Teddy pushed himself closer to Ollie's chest and Ollie wrapped his arms around him and slowly thrust into him, Teddy knew this was forever.

Ollie cared for him. He showed that in how patient he'd been with Teddy, how careful he'd been when he'd prepped him. Foreplay had never lasted so long, and it had driven Teddy crazy. Ollie still was doing that, actually. He was moving inside Teddy slowly, carefully, as if he were afraid of hurting him, and Teddy thought he probably was. He was treating Teddy as if he was made of fragile porcelain. And while Teddy was kind of frustrated with that right now, he was also touched. Ollie didn't want to hurt him, and that meant a lot. Everything Ollie did meant a lot.

Teddy dug his fingernails into Ollie's shoulders. "You can move harder," he murmured, his voice already rough.

Ollie shook his head. "Don't want to hurt you."

"You won't." But it felt so damn good to know that was a reason Ollie was careful. It made Teddy want so much more than what they had right now, even though it was already a lot. He wanted to bond with Ollie.

He knew it was ridiculous. They'd been together for no

121

more than a few months. They were still trying to find their way around each other — to learn each other and how to live together — how to be a couple. They hadn't fought yet, and Teddy found that strange, even though he liked it. He knew they were going to, eventually. But in the meantime, he couldn't help but want even more than what they had.

He would think anyone who wanted to marry the guy they'd been with for two months was crazy, but that was what he was thinking about doing, and he didn't think he was. Maybe it was because they were mates, but that shouldn't change a lot. Yes, it meant that they shared a bond not a lot of people shared, but even though it made them perfect for each other, it didn't make their *relationship* perfect. Teddy should give both of them more time to get used to each other, but he didn't want to. For once in his life, he didn't want to go the rational way. He wanted to act on instinct, and that wasn't like him, and he wasn't sure whether the fact that Ollie brought that out of him was a good thing or a bad one.

He would have thought it was bad only a few months ago, when he had been sure that Ollie would ruin everything he'd worked so hard for, but Teddy was learning to push the little voice that told him to be careful to the back of his head and not listen to it.

He couldn't help but wonder if he should this time, though. The little voice was telling him it was too soon to bond with Ollie, and that he shouldn't act on his feelings. It was right when it came to not biting Ollie without asking for his permission, of course, but Teddy was also terrified that Ollie would say yes. If he asked Ollie to bond, and Ollie agreed, they would have to go through with it, and that thought was both the best thought Teddy had ever had and the most terrifying one. He didn't know what to do with a mate, but he was learning, and he knew that would continue.

"I think I'm doing something wrong," Ollie grunted.

Teddy frowned. "No, you're not."

"But you're not focusing on what we're doing, and in my book, that means I'm doing something wrong."

Teddy chuckled and shook his head. "This is perfect." And it was. Ollie was still moving inside him, but thankfully, he'd accelerated, and it took everything Teddy had not to lose his mind over it. Like always when he felt this way, he retreated in his thoughts, which was why he was focused on whether or not he and Ollie should bond rather than on the sex they were having.

But that needed to change. Teddy would have all the time in the world to think about their bonding after. Right now, he should enjoy the first time he and Ollie had penetrative sex. He wanted to. He just needed to turn his brain off.

One hard thrust from Ollie was enough to make that happen. Teddy yelled and clutched Ollie's shoulders, trying to push his hips closer to his mate, to get Ollie to move deeper inside him. He wanted them to be one, and he didn't know how to make that happen.

Ollie did, though, and he continued to move, holding Teddy close as if he was afraid Teddy was going to disappear. It was slightly uncomfortable, and Ollie was heavy, but Teddy didn't care. As long as he had Ollie around him and inside him, in his heart, he was happy.

Of course, he would also be happy if he could breathe.

He gently pushed Ollie back but stayed wrapped around him. Ollie rose on his elbows, not moving far, but that was enough. Teddy sucked in a deep breath, then pulled Ollie down again and kissed him. He wrapped his legs around the small of Ollie's back and used that hold to thrust up when Ollie thrust down. Ollie shuddered in Teddy's arms, and Teddy lost track of his thoughts.

"What is it?" Ollie asked.

Teddy briefly closed his eyes. "Nothing."

"You're lying."

"I want to bond with you," Teddy blurted out. Apparently, sex got rid of his brain to mouth filter.

Ollie's eyes widened, and he stopped moving. Teddy glared at him because that wouldn't do. "Come on," he said, gently slapping Ollie's back.

Ollie shook his head. "Wait."

"What? Your dick is in my ass, and I was about to come before you stopped moving." Teddy wanted to take himself in hand and jack off until he finally came, but he didn't want to do this alone.

"Do it."

Teddy blinked, wondering how Ollie had managed to read his mind until he realized that wasn't what had happened. "Do what?" he asked cautiously.

"Bite me. Bond us together."

"Are you sure?" This was what Teddy wanted, but he needed to be *a hundred percent* sure it was what Ollie wanted, too. Teddy already knew he'd regret it, at least sometimes. He was just the kind of person who thought about what he'd done again and again, wondering if there was something different that he should have done, but he knew this was forever. That would never change, and it was okay with him. Even if he got angry enough with Ollie that he suddenly wanted to leave, it didn't mean he would love Ollie less.

"I would have bonded with you the first day," Ollie admitted. "The only reason I didn't say anything was that I knew how hesitant you were about a relationship. But now you're saying you want to bond with me, and I'm more than okay with that. So do it. Bite me. Please."

Teddy didn't want to start thinking now. He was already doing more thinking than he was comfortable with in this situation. This was what he and Ollie would end up doing anyway, so instead of obsessing over whether or not this was the right thing to do, he jerked up and sank his fangs into Ollie's neck.

Ollie grunted and finally started moving again. The position was even more awkward when Ollie leaned down and pressed his lips against Teddy's neck, but Teddy didn't care. He was pretty sure he was going to come as soon as Ollie bit him, and that would happen even if Ollie stopped fucking him.

Teddy didn't want to think. He didn't need to.

Ollie's fangs scraped against Teddy's skin, and Teddy had to screw his eyes shut. Pleasure was building in his groin, and he knew he was going to come as soon as Ollie got his fangs into him.

He was right. There was a slight pain, and his entire body seized. He came when Ollie drank the first mouthful of blood, and he almost forgot to seal the wound in Ollie's neck. Ollie's blood tasted like warm copper, but it was special because of what it was doing. It was bonding them together, and that was all Teddy had ever wanted, even though he hadn't known it.

He'd always known he belonged with his brother. That wasn't going to change, but it wasn't the same thing. Jayden had his mate, and Teddy had only had Jayden. That had changed when he'd met Ollie, and now, Teddy had someone of his own, someone who would always be his, and only his. He belonged somewhere, truly belonged, and even though he hadn't known it, this was what he'd been looking for forever.

The bond snapped into place, and Teddy was finally complete. It wasn't like Ollie was something Teddy had been missing, but his presence in the back of Teddy's mind was soothing, and it helped Teddy not start obsessing over what they'd done. In any other situation, he would already be brushing his orgasm off and thinking about all the consequences the bond would have, but he didn't now. He couldn't have, even if he'd tried.

He was exhausted, and as soon as Ollie licked the blood clean from his neck, he flopped onto the mattress. Ollie chuckled, and Teddy hoped his mate had come, because he wasn't sure he could move right now.

"You're tired," Ollie said.

Teddy rolled his eyes. "What makes you think so?"

Ollie settled into bed next to Teddy, propped up on his elbow as he looked down at Teddy and ran his fingers over Teddy's stomach. Teddy's semen was still there, and Ollie was making a mess, but Teddy couldn't bring himself to care about it. "I was surprised," Ollie murmured.

"That I wanted to bond with you?" Teddy asked, even though he didn't have to. He knew that had surprised Ollie. It had surprised even himself.

Ollie nodded. "Yeah. I thought it would take us a long time to get to this point. I hope you won't regret it."

Teddy hated that Ollie thought he would, so he hooked a hand around Ollie's neck and pulled him down to kiss him. "I'll never regret *you*. I'll never regret being with you. There's not much I'm sure of in my life, but this, I do know. You're it for me, Ollie. Whatever happens with the rest of the world and the rest of our lives, we'll always have each other." And that meant so much to Teddy.

He might not be ready to tell Ollie he loved him, but then, he hadn't told anyone he loved them in so many years, and maybe he just wasn't capable of doing it anymore. But Ollie knew Teddy loved him. Teddy knew Ollie loved him, too. He could feel it clearly through the bond, and while it was going to take some time to get used to, he couldn't wait to see what happened next.

You may also enjoy the following from eXtasy Books Inc:

Davis
Catherine Lievens

Excerpt

Davis Calvin was mortified. He wanted to die.

He tried to extricate himself from the man's beard, but he was stuck, the hair wrapping around his paws and arms.

What the fuck had happened?

Calvin knew the answer to that. What had happened was that he'd shifted without meaning to, just like always. What had happened was that he'd been in the middle of the hallway, and he'd tried to go back into the breakroom, but he hadn't managed before this guy came out of the bathroom. He was desperate to get away. He didn't want to be close to the man, whoever he was. He didn't want to be close to anyone. He was terrified that this guy would tell Nate that he was a shifter, and he didn't know what to do about that. He didn't know how to explain.

He tried to pull again, but he couldn't break free. Maybe it was time for him to learn how to fly, but how was he supposed to do that when he had no one to teach him. He didn't know how to be a bat shifter. He was pretty sure there were at least a few bat shifters in the pack, but going to them would mean letting people know what he was, and he wasn't ready for that. He wasn't ready for Nate to find out.

It felt like the more he tried to pull free, the more tangled he became in the beard. He pulled and pulled, but he couldn't get free.

Then two large hands cupped him, and he froze.

"Good boy," the man crooned. "Or are you a girl? I don't know how to see the difference, I'm sorry. Did you come from outside?" The man's voice was soothing. Calvin wasn't sure why, but it made him want to bury himself deeper into the man's soft beard instead of getting free, which was ridiculous.

The man's behavior had helped Calvin calm down, and now he realized that he shouldn't pull on the beard to get free. That wouldn't help. Just like it had before, it would only entangle him deeper into the hair, and that was the last thing both him and this guy wanted.

Calvin forced himself to calm down. He breathed in and out, and that was when the smell hit him.

It made the world around him tilt sideways. He didn't know what it meant, and he didn't want to think about it right now.

He stayed still while the man gently untangled, but when Calvin tried to fly away as soon as he was free—and he wasn't sure he could—the man cupped his hands around him again and held him close. Calvin panicked and tried to break out of the hold, but the man didn't let go, and Calvin tangled into his beard again. Instead of getting angry, the man soothed Calvin's fur, stroking his big fingers onto it, and even though he didn't know what was happening, Calvin relaxed. The man's hands were gentle, and his touch was everything Calvin had been yearning for even though he hadn't known it.

The man finished untangling his beard from Calvin's claws, then gently raised him until they could look at each other in the eyes. Calvin blinked and tried to get out of the man's hands, but again, he didn't let go.

Calvin bit him.

It didn't matter how gentle this man was, he needed to get away. He couldn't allow Nate to find out what he was. He couldn't allow Nate to see how much he'd changed. Calvin couldn't be vulnerable, no matter how much he wanted to stay close to the man.

The man yelped and opened his hands, and Calvin flew away. Or at least, he tried to fly away. He'd always sucked at flying, and he suspected that was mostly because he hadn't been allowed to. Even now, he wasn't allowing himself to try because he couldn't let anyone find out what he was. That meant that instead of flying to the breakroom like he'd meant to, he flapped his wings a few times, then plummeted to the floor. He hit it fast, and pain exploded in his wings. He prayed nothing was broken because he needed to get out of here.

Since he couldn't fly, he tried to drag himself toward the door. In the meantime, he was also trying to shift back to his human form, even though it was probably the worst thing he could do right now. This guy, whoever he was, thought that Calvin was a wild bat. Maybe if Calvin allowed him to take him, he would release him outside. That way, the guy wouldn't find out that Calvin was a shifter.

Of course, Calvin had no idea what he'd do if he had to fly around as a bad. He was pretty sure that something would try to eat him, and they would probably succeed.

Warm fingers wrapped around his body again. "Don't bite me again, please. I'm just trying to help you," the man said. His voice was a whisper, and again, Calvin relaxed.

What was it with this guy's voice? With his scent? Calvin should try to run away, but instead, he found himself snuggling into the man's hands, trying to get closer. What was wrong with him? Why was he reacting this way?

The man pulled Calvin closer again. "I promise I'm not trying to hurt you," he murmured. "I just want to get you outside so you can fly home."

Calvin rolled his eyes. As if he could fly anywhere.

The man's eyes widened. "Okay. I'm pretty sure that wild bats aren't supposed to roll their eyes the way you just did. Does that mean you're a shifter, little guy?"

Shit. Calvin was giving himself out, and he couldn't allow that to happen. He didn't want to bite the man again, though, and he held his breath as the man brought him even closer to his face, until their noses almost touched.

The man took a deep breath, and Calvin hadn't thought it possible, but his eyes widened even more.

The man looked so shocked that Calvin expected him to drop him. What the fuck was going on?

"Well, I can't say I expected this to happen," the man said. He stroked a finger down Calvin's back. "And I don't think you expected this to happen, either. Do you think you can shift back? We should probably talk or at the very least, exchange phone numbers."

Calvin blinked. What was this man talking about?"

Calvin decided to try to get away again because this guy didn't seem to be all there in his head. He was gentle enough, but Calvin didn't need to be involved in this, whatever this was.

But of course, the man didn't let him go. He wasn't harsh when he kept Calvin in his hands, and that was a relief. But he was also not freeing Calvin, and Calvin wasn't sure what to do about that.

"Don't panic. It's okay. I know it's a surprise, and that's okay. I don't expect anything from you, not right now," the man said.

Calvin wanted to shift to ask him what the fuck he was talking about, but no matter how hard he tried, he couldn't manage. He still had no idea how to control the shifts, which was why he was flying in the hallway of his brother's bar as a bat instead of walking around as a human. He needed to get upstairs and lock himself in his bedroom. Nate would understand. He'd think Calvin had been overwhelmed, and he would leave him alone. Hopefully, it would be long enough for Calvin to shift back into his human form.

But first, he had to get away from this guy, no matter how nice he smelled.

The man raised Calvin again, and this time, he was frowning. "I don't understand. Why are you trying to run away from me?" He paused and smiled, and God, how he was so gorgeous. Calvin had always had a type — bigger than him so he could feel protected, rugged but gentle — and that hadn't changed, even though he hadn't let anyone else close since he'd come back. He needed to be protected even more than before, even though it made him feel weak.

"Okay, it's obvious that something is wrong, even though I don't understand what," the man said. He looked around. "Maybe I should find someone who knows who you are?"

Calvin reared back. Was this guy a friend of Nate's? Calvin had thought he'd seen all of them, but then, he'd only started coming down to the bar over the past few weeks. Nate had a lot of friends.

And this guy was an enforcer. He wore the uniform, and he wore it well. It made Calvin want to bury against him, possibly without clothes on, but he couldn't. He needed to shift back, but he had no idea how.

"Okay. Let's do this. I'm going to take you to the bar, okay? We'll find someone who can help since I obviously can't."

Calvin's heart raced. He tried to fly away again, but he should have known better. He couldn't fly. He'd never been able to.

He tripped out of the man's hands and fell, and he closed his eyes as the floor came closer.

ABOUT THE AUTHOR

Catherine is the creator of several series, most of them paranormal, including the Whitedell Pride Series and the Gillham Pack Series. While she graduated in translation, she decided to go the writer's way because it was more fun to create her own stories and characters.

She's been living in Italy for more than twenty years, but she's a daughter of the North—Belgium to be precise—and she misses it so much that she's already planning to move back.

She loves pizza—probably too much—her pets, and of course, books. She sneaks some reading time in her schedule every time she has five minutes free from writing, demands from her various pets and son, and lastly, housework.

Connect with her:

lievens.catherine@gmail.com
BookBub
Website
Facebook
Facebook Group
Twitter
Newsletter

www.ingramcontent.com/pod-product-compliance
Lightning Source LLC
Chambersburg PA
CBHW060623130626
46555CB00002B/630

* 9 7 8 1 4 8 7 4 2 7 9 8 6 *